THE HAUNTING OF HILLWOOD FARM

KATHRYN KNIGHT

Wicked Whale
Publishing

Knight, Kathryn

The Haunting of Hillwood Farm / by Kathryn Knight

Summary: When a reluctant psychic agrees to investigate a haunting, she finds a chance at love, even as she becomes the target of a vengeful spirit.

ISBN: 978-1-7322522-3-3

Wicked Whale Publishing
P.O. Box 264
Sagamore Beach, MA 02562-9998

www.WickedWhalePublishing.com

Published in the United States of America

"I clung to my tablet and couldn't look away. If you're looking for spooky romantic suspense, you'll love The Haunting of Hillwood Farm. Kathryn Knight has mastered the art of paranormal romantic suspense and it's a must-read. 5+ stars."

~ N.N. Light's Book Heaven on The Haunting of Hillwood Farm

"In Gull Harbor, the author skillfully weaves the ghost story and romance from separate strands that eventually become entangled. There's a perfect blending of clues, hints, and foreshadowing, but the story never veers into the obvious or predictable. Pace, plot, story, dialog, and characters combine into a thrilling and thoroughly entertaining page-turner."

~ My Shelf Reviews on Gull Harbor

"Every character in Silver Lake is perfectly developed. I could not put this book down. Romance, drama, renewal of friendships, and ghosts...something for everyone. I cannot wait to see what Kathryn Knight writes next!"

~ A Novel Review on Silver Lake

To Kathy, my friend, cheerleader, and Beta Reader ~ for always being willing to dive into every chapter, for your careful proof-reads, and for supporting me through every step of this journey. Thank you for everything.

CHAPTER 1

*T*he sugar bowl slid across the kitchen counter, its lid rattling with jerky bursts of motion. Alice Turner froze, her fingers clenched around the mug of coffee she held suspended in midair, a curl of steam wavering in the sudden chill. Goosebumps prickled her skin as she stared at the yellow ceramic bowl, zigzagging its way toward her via some unseen force. It jittered to a halt directly in front of her, and her taut muscles went limp. Her coffee mug slammed down against the dark stone countertop, sending scalding liquid sloshing over her hand. She cried out, more from fright than pain, and stumbled back, nearly tripping as her foot slid out of its slipper. The near fall sent another bolt of panic through her. At 73, she was still quite active, but a broken bone would put an end to that.

She steadied herself. *Careful.* Blowing out a breath, she glanced at the reddening skin of her hand before quickly returning her gaze to the wayward bowl. *Had it really just moved on its own?* Despite the fear coursing through her veins, a wave of relief washed over her.

Maybe she *wasn't* losing her mind. Maybe all her recent worries about dementia, fueled by things like finding objects someplace other than where she'd left them, or discovering kitchen drawers open when she was sure she'd closed them, were unfounded. Could some kind of...supernatural phenomenon be responsible? A shiver crawled up her spine. That alternative wasn't a particularly comforting thought. And her practical New England roots didn't exactly lend themselves to that line of reasoning.

She cradled her throbbing hand against her chest, studying the sugar bowl for more movement. But it seemed to have completed its journey and had now reverted to an inanimate object, ready and waiting to sweeten her coffee.

With cautious steps, she backed away from the counter, crossing the kitchen toward the sink. Flipping on the faucet, she held her injured hand under the stream of cold water.

Was she really considering the presence of a ghost? It would help to explain all the strange occurrences she'd noticed since she'd returned from her trip. Without Henry. A deep ache flared in her chest as her gaze cut over to the chair he used to settle in at the big farmhouse table, empty now. With a heavy sigh, she glanced back at the stationary bowl as she dried her hand with a checkered dish towel.

It *had* moved. She was certain. Retrieving her mug, she nodded forcefully, trying to push away the pinpricks of doubt threatening to erode her conviction. Either a spirit had manipulated the sugar bowl, or she was truly cracking up. The latter theory felt like the more terrifying one. She didn't even want to contemplate the possibility that her ties to sanity, already frayed by grief, had finally snapped, and hallucinations were her new reality.

Maybe it was time to talk to Luke, to see if he'd noticed anything unusual since he'd been living with her at Hillwood. It was just that he was already so worried about her. As much as she loved him, she didn't need a babysitter; nor did she want her 27-year-old grandson to have to take on that role. So far, their cohabitation was working out, but once he got a load of her sugar bowl story, that might change quickly.

Another pocket of frigid air swirled around her, and she spun around. Her gaze searched the empty kitchen and the back hallway. No one was there. She turned back slowly, her heart thumping in her ears. From her position behind the long counter separating the kitchen from the dining room, she could see the foyer. The front door remained shut. The windows were still closed against last night's rain. Besides that, it was 65 degrees outside, according to the thermometer in the window above the sink. A cold front inside the house made little sense, unless...

"Henry?" Her voice wavered in the silence.

The sugar bowl shivered slightly, as if a small earthquake had opened up beneath it. An extremely localized earthquake that had no effect on anything else nearby. Her trembling hands flew to her mouth as a potent mix of fear and longing swept through her. She slid her damp palms downward, over the hammering in her chest. "Is that you?" she added, the words barely emerging from her dusty throat.

The lights flickered. She glanced up, her breath catching. A soft moan rippled through the air, raising in pitch until it became a distant wail. She clutched the folds of her robe, every muscle in her body vibrating with tension. A sudden movement caught her eye, and she snapped her head back toward the sugar bowl as it careened off the counter, shattering in an explosion of ceramic shards and white powder.

CHAPTER 2

*T*he farmhouse looked completely normal from the outside, if a little worse for the wear due to its age. According to Alice, the historic home in Sandwich, Massachusetts, had been in the Turner family not just for generations but for centuries, with parts of the original 1780s structure still intact amongst the additions and renovations completed over the years. A wide, welcoming porch, complete with Adirondack chairs, rockers, and hanging plants, stretched across the front of the home, wrapping around the sides. Old steel milk jugs flanked the red front door, and checkered curtains hung in the windows. Everything about it was quaint and inviting.

But Callie Sinclair felt it as soon as they climbed the worn wooden steps to the porch. *Something was here.* Sure enough, when Alice opened the front door and gestured her inside, the whispers began. They swirled through her head, a chorus of faraway voices rustling like tattered leaves in the wind, traveling through time and space, from who knew where.

Despite the warmth of the early May afternoon, a shiver slid through her, and she pulled her long, light-weight sweater coat around her chest, resisting the urge to try to close off her mind. She was here to listen, after all, and she could feel the nervous anticipation rolling off of Alice as they entered the foyer. The older woman had clearly been excited for her arrival; she'd met Callie in the long driveway, her silvery hair catching in the spring breeze as strands escaped the knot pinned loosely on the back of her head.

"Are you cold, dear?" The furrows lining Alice's fore-head deepened. "Or do you...feel something?"

"Just a little chill," she said with a weak smile, purpose-fully keeping her answer vague. She did feel something beyond a mysterious chill in the air...but she didn't want to get Alice's hopes up. And it was difficult to explain. Of course there were remnants of past lives lingering here; it was pretty much a given for any home with this type of history. Many people connected to this house would have passed on over the years, leaving some imprint of their essence, like the blurred images captured beneath closed eyelids after a bright flash.

But she was here to connect with someone specific: Henry Turner. Alice had sought Callie out upon hearing about her abilities from a mutual acquaintance. When Callie had reluctantly agreed to meet Alice at a coffee shop last week, she'd taken pity on the kind widow. How could she not? Alice and Henry had been married 53 years, and they had saved up to finally afford their dream vacation—a 28-day Polynesian cruise. When Henry had suffered a massive heart attack in the middle of the South Pacific Ocean, the medical personnel on board had not been able to save him.

But after the funeral, when things began settling down at the normally quiet farmhouse, Alice started noticing strange occurrences, which increased in frequency and severity as the weeks went by. She now firmly believed her late husband was trying to tell her something—and that his message was urgent.

Callie hadn't wanted to get involved, but Alice truly seemed to believe she—or someone she loved—might be in danger, and contact with Henry was the key to possibly preventing tragedy. Either Alice was genuinely concerned, or she was an excellent actress… but Callie couldn't see the point in making a story like that up, considering Alice would be paying her money for her services. When Alice's pleas were joined by barely contained tears, Callie relented.

And now, here she was. In an isolated old farmhouse, with a woman she really didn't know, searching for a ghost.

While she could hear the lingering murmurs of long-gone souls, she couldn't make out anything distinct. So far, there was no bright spark of connection to a specific person, like she'd experienced before. But maybe she just needed to give it time. What did she know about the process, really? The few times it had happened to her, the spirits had come to her, on their own, and had plagued her with a determined tenacity until she opened her mind up to the messages and relayed them to the intended recipients. If there was a process she was supposed to go through, she had no idea what it was. She had no degree in this type of thing, no certification. It was just a bizarre and unwelcome result of the accident.

"I feel it from time to time too," Alice said, a knowing look gleaming in her pale blue eyes. She closed the front door to block the air coming in through the screen door and nodded toward the kitchen. "How about a cup of hot coffee? Or tea?"

"I never say no to coffee," she said gratefully, playing with the long dragonfly pendant around her neck. That was true, although she'd probably had enough already this morning at her apartment.

She was starting to think coming here was a mistake. But Alice had been so desperate, and Callie herself knew how comforting a message from beyond could be. That first time, though, right after the accident, she'd thought she was losing her mind. But then it started happening again, whenever she was with Karen, her physical therapist, and she finally gathered up the nerve to ask her if she had a sister who'd died recently. And the answer, sadly, had been a surprised 'yes'. Once Callie began relaying the phrases echoing through her head, things Karen confirmed only the twin sisters would have known, her new reality set in. And Karen avoided marrying the fiancé who was cheating on her. After a few more instances, Callie came to accept she was now some kind of conduit between two worlds—but she'd never actively sought the connection before. Maybe if you tried to force it, it wouldn't come.

Still playing with her necklace, a gift from her father, she followed Alice into the house. The floorplan was open on either side of the central staircase, with a welcoming family room to the left; they walked to the right, through an airy dining area that transitioned into the kitchen. The décor was a mix of country charm and seaside accents, a nod to both their rural homestead and its location on Cape Cod, a peninsula surrounded by water. Old signs advertising fruits and vegetables for sale hung on the pale yellow walls, and canning jars filled with shells sat on the windowsills.

Part of the counter top extended out in an L-shape between the kitchen and dining spaces, and Callie leaned against it, admiring an antique-looking iron rooster tucked in the corner. *Did they have hens here?* Fresh eggs every morning would be such a luxury. She'd noticed a few other buildings at the bottom of the hill beyond the house, one of which looked like a barn. But the only animal she'd seen thus far was a large black cat, sitting on a post of a split rail fence and eyeing her with contempt.

"I know it's the afternoon already, but is a breakfast blend okay?" Alice asked as she filled the coffee pot in the deep white sink. "My grandson likes the stronger stuff, so I do have dark roast."

"Breakfast blend sounds wonderful."

Alice measured the coffee, then gestured with the little metal scoop toward where Callie stood. "That's where the sugar bowl slid off the counter and smashed."

Her gaze found a new sugar bowl, next to a napkin holder resembling chicken wire, and Callie stared at it for a moment, as if history might repeat itself.

Alice retrieved two mugs from an overhead cabinet. "I know it sounds crazy, but I saw it with my own two eyes, even if they are old eyes."

"I believe you." She reached for the sugar bowl herself, moving it within easy reach. "Is there anything I can do to help?"

Alice waved her offer away as she crossed to the fridge and pulled out a jug of milk. "No, no, just make yourself comfortable." She poured some milk into a small white pitcher and picked up the thread of the previous conversation. "Even if I'd had any doubt about it moving on its own, I sure didn't imagine cleaning up all the mess after it flew off the edge and hit the floor."

Callie nodded as she pulled a stool from under the counter. "That must have been a frustrating way to start the morning."

"The thing is...why would Henry want to make me have to clean up a big mess?" Alice set the milk pitcher next to the sugar bowl, locking her gaze with Callie's. Her thin lips pressed into a seam, turning the soft folds of skin around her mouth into parenthesis. The coffee maker sputtered and gurgled in the background. "He was always telling me I was doing too much around here, after I hurt my shoulder. I mean, we had disagreements on occasion, just like any couple, but I have no doubt he loved me. In the 53 years we were together, he was never mean-spirited or cruel."

Callie frowned, a small sound of acknowledgement

emerging from the back of her throat. It was an interesting observation, but she certainly didn't have the answer. *Go on, then, Henry...explain. I'm listening.*

"When it first started moving, a small part of my brain thought, 'He's trying to help me, to pass the sugar'. It was scary, but a little sweet. But then when it suddenly smashed like that, it felt...different. Not sweet anymore. It felt...angry."

"I'm sure it's hard for a spirit to move something in the physical world. Maybe he just...doesn't have a lot of control over it," she offered, shifting on her stool as she gathered her dark curtain of hair over her shoulder and coiled it into a rope.

Alice tilted her head to the side, considering. "Well, he certainly got my attention, if that was the point. And then there were all the other things that have happened that I told you about last week. The family pictures that fell and shattered after years of hanging on the same wall. A huge crack appearing in my car's windshield when it was safely in the garage. All the laundry I'd hung on the clothesline ending up on the ground. Important papers going missing." She ticked off each incident on her thin fingers, the gold band on her left hand catching the light from the fixture overhead. With a small shrug, she added, "Anyway, all this was enough to convince me to find someone who could help, that's for sure." She nodded toward Callie before turning back toward the coffee maker.

Of course, it remained to be seen whether she could actually be any help. A surge of nervous energy hummed through her, and she ordered herself to relax. There was no real pressure here; she had signed no contract, received no money. She'd only agreed to come by the house for an initial visit, and go from there.

Danger. The word rustled in her head, thick and muffled, as though coming from underwater. But it wasn't her thought, and it was accompanied by that familiar flare of pressure in her skull. She froze, her eyes searching the room. She'd never actually seen a ghost, but the instinct to look for a figure to go with a disembodied voice was tough to ignore.

Nothing but the back of Alice's thin but surprisingly sturdy frame as she filled two coffee mugs on the other side of the kitchen. Cropped tan pants, untucked powder blue blouse, pewter strands of hair still vying for freedom from the loose bun.

She turned her head slowly. Just the vacant farm table, the empty foyer, and a partial view of the front door, still closed.

A tremor shuddered through her. So...a connection had been made, even if briefly. And the message—*danger*—was not exactly comforting. Knitting her brows, she strained to pick up something else. But it was just the background noise of whispers now, slowly fading away like a battery draining of power. Those spirits had no real reason to reach her, no unfinished business keeping them caught between worlds. They only wanted someone to know they'd been here, once, and had left a tiny piece of their presence behind. The memory of a life lived.

Ghosts who moved things in the physical world and sought out mediums, in her experience anyway, had something important to relay. And the fact that someone—Alice?—was in danger...well, that felt important. Callie realized she was stuck now. How could she refuse to help if danger lurked around this sweet woman?

The thud of footsteps on the porch jolted her from her ruminations, and she jumped in her seat, the word *danger* still rattling through her mind.

CHAPTER 3

*H*er heart slammed against her ribcage as she whipped her head back and forth between the closed front door and her hostess. Alice was frozen in the middle of the kitchen, her eyes wide with something like concern, her mouth rounded into a small O.

Who was here? Before Callie could even think what to do, the door opened, and a man entered. A baseball cap shaded his face, so she couldn't tell if his expression was menacing or pleasant. When he didn't lunge toward them, she relaxed a few degrees, but her blood still thumped in her ears. They were two women, alone in an isolated house, and this man looked like he could do some damage if he wanted to. He was tall and broad-shouldered, the hard muscles of his arms exposed by a gray short-sleeved T-shirt. Beneath worn jeans, he wore heavy work boots that echoed against the wooden floorboards as he turned to shut the door.

"Oh, Luke, you surprised me. I thought you had a

meeting in Plymouth." Alice snapped out of her momentary stupor, but her words seemed laced with forced casualness.

Luke? It took Callie another beat to make the connection, but then she remembered. Alice had mentioned her grandson was living with her in the farmhouse for the time being, while he fixed up another building on the property to serve as his own place. Apparently, he hadn't wanted his grandmother to be at Hillwood all alone after Henry had suddenly passed away, and he'd moved into one of the home's guest rooms after putting his own house on the market.

A surge of warmth wound through her at the thought of that kind of selfless protectiveness, but she steeled herself against it. *I don't even know this man.* It had been obvious during their initial meeting how Alice felt about her grandson, her voice vibrating with love and pride as she'd explained their current living situation. But God knew relatives did horrible things to each other; all the true crime shows on TV were proof of that. And for some reason, Alice now looked like she'd been caught doing something wrong.

Could the mysterious "danger" warning have something to do with Luke Turner? Tiny hairs prickled along the back of her neck.

"I did," he replied. "But he called while I was on the way, some kind of personal emergency." Luke strode into the dining room, removing his hat and raking his free hand through thick, light brown hair.

Whoa. Her stomach did a little flip. He was strikingly

15

handsome. She shifted on the stool, her fingers plucking at a patch of frayed denim in the fashionably ripped skinny jeans she'd bought on sale.

"So I just ran a few errands," Luke finished, resting a hand on the back of a chair. He flicked a curious glance between his grandmother and Callie.

"Oh." Alice shook her head as if to clear it. "This is Callie. Callie, this is my grandson, Luke," she added, sliding one of the full coffee mugs across the counter.

Once again, the affection Alice felt for her grandson rang clear in her introductions. Callie pulled in a breath and offered Luke a smile, battling against a nervous twitch pulsing in the corner of her mouth. *What was wrong with her?* "Hi," she managed.

His gaze swept over her, lingered. He nodded. "Nice to meet you." He leaned forward, extending his hand.

A warm flush crept up her neck, spreading to her cheeks. Good Lord. Dangerous or not, he was just so...hot. His looks were muddling her thoughts, that was all. But a strange thrill ran through her, and she suddenly realized she hadn't felt any kind of attraction toward a man since Andrew. As she slipped her hand into his, her skin tingled pleasantly, as though her body was trying to prove its point.

His full lips curved into a slow, sexy smile, revealing small dimples beneath the slight scruff of whiskers that hadn't seen a razor that morning. He cocked his brows, a quizzical look flickering in his steel blue eyes, and she realized he was probably waiting for further explanation as to who the heck she was. Alice hadn't specified their relationship, and there was certainly a large age gap between the two women. Callie was 25, probably just a bit younger than Luke; random friendship seemed an unlikely scenario.

She glanced toward his grandmother for help, but all Alice said was, "I just made coffee. Can I get you a cup?"

"That sounds great. But I'll get it, Gram. You sit down."

Alice waved him away, crossing back to the other side of the kitchen. "I'm fine."

He turned his attention back to Callie. "So...are you looking to board a horse?"

She blinked, still struggling to regain her bearings after everything that had happened in the last five minutes. "No, I'm—" Out of the corner of her vision, she caught Alice giving her the slightest shake of her head, and she cut herself off. "Um...I don't have a horse," she finished lamely.

His forehead crinkled, eyes narrowing. He studied her, realization dawning across his chiseled features like a lengthening shadow. Cords tightened along the sides of his neck as his expression turned hard. "Wait." He swiveled toward Alice. "Gram, tell me this has nothing to do with Pop."

"Now, hang on a moment, Luke," Alice said, the words rushing out, her tone a cross between defensive and flustered. "I told you what's been going on. You've seen the damage yourself. I invited her here."

He accepted the mug of coffee Alice pushed into his hands, transferring it directly to the table without taking his eyes off Callie. "How much money have you scammed off a grieving widow so far?"

Beneath his glare, her insides twisted. "What?" Indignation rose along with her voice. "Look, I haven't asked for or accepted any kind of payment."

Alice cut in again, her cheeks glowing pink. "It's true. I tried to offer her money to come here, but she refused. Although I *am* going to insist on paying her if she can help figure out what's going on here."

A muscle in his jaw twitched. "So, you bill yourself as some kind of psychic or something?" He folded his arms over his chest, biceps bunching, tendons taut.

Squaring her shoulders, she pulled in a breath. "I don't 'bill myself' as anything," she replied hotly. *Good God, I did not sign up for this.*

"Okay," Alice interrupted, waving her hand in the air like a flag. "This isn't conducive to...anything. I'm the one that searched out Callie and asked her to come here. Begged her, really, because at first, she didn't want to get involved. So now that she's here, I'd like to see if she feels anything."

I'm feeling a lot of things, actually. Callie bit down on her lip to keep the sarcasm in. If she hadn't already heard that warning message, she'd be out of here. But she had, and now she was, as Alice put it, 'involved'. She sighed inwardly.

Sipping her coffee, Alice continued her quest to calm the waters. "Maybe a tour of the property would be helpful, Callie. Henry spent a lot of time down at the barn or the other outbuildings. He loved it here." Her expression grew wistful as she gazed out the kitchen window. A birdfeeder hung on the other side of the glass, secured by suction cups, and a pair of sparrows flitted around it. Sunlight spilled across the floor.

Luke finally broke the moment of silence. "Gram, your shoulder is still healing. I'll take her around." His last sentence carried the weight of a painful chore.

Alice made a dismissive noise, waving his concern away. "It's a walk, not hauling around hay bales. I'll be fine. But we'd love to have you along."

We would? Callie pressed her teeth a little harder into her bottom lip, sending up a tiny flare of pain.

"I'll just get a jacket, it's a little breezy out. Callie, will you be okay?"

Callie glanced down at her outfit. A thin ivory sweater coat served as her outerwear, layered over an emerald camisole she liked because it highlighted the green of her eyes. The sweater's knit was loose, exposing tiny dots of skin along her arms, but it was long-sleeved. "I think I'll be fine." When she looked up, she caught Luke's gaze on her as well, his eyes quickly sliding away from the swell of cleavage revealed by her low-cut cami. Flushing, she stood, pulling the sweater across her chest.

Alice motioned to the hall extending from the back of the kitchen. "Okay. There's a bathroom back here, too, Callie. I'll be out in just a minute if you need to use it, but there's one in the barn as well." She hurried out of the kitchen, and a door in the back hallway clicked shut.

Callie's coffee mug was still nearly full, and she reached for it, hoping she appeared less uncomfortable than she felt, alone here with Luke. At least she'd noticed a slight ruddy stain rise across his cheekbones after she'd caught him checking her out. It evened the playing field a little. She just wished her body hadn't responded with the warm rush of desire still swirling low in her belly. But he didn't have to know that. It was just that it had been so long… there'd been no one since Andrew. She hadn't even tried. Who in their right mind would want to get involved with her the way she was now, anyway?

Luke cleared his throat, lifting his own mug. "I don't believe in this stuff, you know."

She shrugged. "Neither did I." If he only knew what she'd been through after the accident. How hard it had been to accept this…odd and terrible "gift".

He frowned as confusion swept over his face. "Well, if you're hoping there's some big inheritance…there's not."

"Okay." *What about you?* Maybe there really was some big inheritance, and he wanted to get rid of Alice so he could get his hands on it. *Danger.* It felt a bit far-fetched, unless he was an amazing actor—she could literally feel the love between the two of them. Then again, psychopaths were probably excellent actors, and it was too early to dismiss anything yet.

Why, then, was she headed out to explore the grounds of this secluded property with him? Well, at least Alice would be with them as well.

Shaking his head, he dragged a hand over his mouth. "I just don't like this," he said, almost to himself.

"I did get that impression."

To her surprise, his lips twitched into the hint of a suppressed smile. Picking up his coffee, he took a swig. "I'll probably try to talk her out of this tonight."

She nodded. "That's fine. Although based on what I've seen of your grandmother so far, she seems a bit stubborn."

This time he actually laughed, his blue eyes glinting with humor and exasperation. "You have no idea."

Alice bustled into the kitchen, pulling on her jacket. Pausing mid-stride, she glanced between the two of them as they laughed, and something passed across her face quickly, like a lightbulb flashing on. "Well, are we ready then? There's a bit more coffee, if anyone wants a refill. I can put it in a travel mug."

She declined politely, even as Luke chuckled again, shaking his head. "Gram, you're making it sound like we're going on a day-long trek." He turned to Callie with a smile, his dimples flashing. "The barn is really not that far away. I think we'll be okay."

Another unbidden surge of heat flowed through her as she returned the smile. *Damn her traitorous hormones.* "Great," she replied, plucking her sunglasses from her small bag. Fortunately, she'd worn low-heeled ankle boots; even if it wasn't a long walk, spikey heels would have made navigating the sloping hills and dirt paths difficult.

Alice adjusted the collar of her beige jacket with exaggerated movements in response to Luke's teasing, shooting a look of feigned annoyance at him as she marched by.

"Aww, Gram, you know I love you," Luke said, turning to wrap a muscular arm around her. With his free hand, he snagged his hat from the chair, and together the two of them walked toward the front door, side by side, Luke towering over his grandmother by at least a foot.

Callie's throat tightened as she watched them cross the

dining room, Alice tucked into Luke's side. So sweet. Her mind took the thought down another path as she suddenly found herself wondering what it would feel like to be wrapped in that protective embrace, and she fought the invasive pull of longing that came with it. Still, she allowed herself a few more seconds to admire his retreating figure, catching the corner of her bottom lip with her teeth.

Cold air swirled around her, and something hard and pointed jabbed her in the middle of her back, sending her stumbling forward. "Ow!" she cried, grabbing onto the chair at the head of the dining table to keep from falling. Spinning around, she searched the space where she'd been standing as she pressed her back protectively against the rungs of the chair.

Empty. There was no one there.

CHAPTER 4

"Callie! Are you all right?" Alice hurried back toward her, concern clouding her features. "What happened?"

She stretched her arm up her back, bending her elbow awkwardly as she tried to rub the lingering ache between her shoulder blades. The spot tingled, simultaneously hot and cold, as though someone had applied a blob of one of those creams for sore muscles. With a single jab of a sharp stick.

"I…" She faltered. The instinct to lie was strong; it was the pattern she'd fallen into after the accident, to avoid strange looks. But, Alice had brought her here for a reason, and she was going to have to start sharing some things for this to work. Swallowing hard, she dropped her arm. "It felt like someone poked me. In the middle of my back."

Behind Alice, Luke rolled his eyes as he pulled his hat on, skepticism nearly radiating off him. "Justifying your billable hours?"

Anger flared. "No," she snapped. "I said I wouldn't take any money unless I could help. Getting poked in the back doesn't seem very helpful." She actually *did* want to help. She certainly had the time, with the way things were going with the rest of her life. And now she sort of wanted to prove to Luke that she wasn't a fraud.

Hesitating, she bit back the urge to tell him about the forbidding message she'd received right before he came in. But he probably wouldn't believe her, and anyway, she didn't want to open herself up to any additional ridicule. She'd tell Alice about it later, after they had walked around a bit. Hopefully she'd have something more to relay at that point.

Alice tossed a glare in Luke's direction as she murmured, "I believe you," rubbing Callie's shoulder gently. "Do you want me to take a look at your back?"

She shook her head. "I'm fine. Should we get on with the tour?" Forcing a weak smile, she gestured toward the front door.

Tugging at the brim of his cap, Luke frowned at her as they made their way into the hall. "Why would my grand-father's ghost want to poke you in the back? Pop was a nice guy."

"Luke," Alice cut in, an undercurrent of warning beneath her cheerful tone. "Why don't you give Callie some of the history of the farm?" It was a command, not a suggestion, and Alice pulled the door closed with a bang to emphasize her point.

"Right." He led them down the porch steps and along the walkway. It connected with the winding driveway she'd ascended as she drove in, and a dusty black pick-up truck now sat beside her car in the wide paved area by the side of the house. A two-car garage had been tacked on a little farther back, clearly a more modern necessity, but care had been taken to preserve the view from the living room windows.

She paused to take it in again. The grassy hill on which the house was situated sloped down here to a sparkling lake that stretched back toward the distant tree line. To the right of the water, white split rail fences encircled wide pastures, and two horses grazed by the far side of one, near the woods. An appreciative sound escaped as she admired the picturesque landscape. "Wow, this is all part of the farm? The lake, too?"

"It is," Luke confirmed, settling his hands on his hips. "Although technically, that's a kettle pond, formed by glaciers. The pond covers five acres, and then there's all the woods, too." He motioned toward the vast expanse of trees surrounding the fields. "The entire property is 27 acres total. The Turners go back to the Mayflower, and this farm has belonged to the family since the late 1700s. For a long time, it was a working farm, generating income from the sale of local fruits and vegetables and hay. It hasn't been profitable in that regard for a while now, but we've managed to stay afloat by getting help from my dad's business."

"It's beautiful." A warm breeze lifted her hair, and she tucked it back behind an ear. "What does your father do?" she asked as the three of them resumed walking.

"He's an attorney. He and my brother have a practice

together now."

"My son John is very successful," Alice added, her voice tinged with both pride and something like resignation. "He never cared much for rural living or manual labor, though, which is why Henry and I didn't move somewhere else and leave the farm to him. He wasn't really interested in living here, and when he got married, well, his wife Cynthia wouldn't even consider it." Shaking her head, she sniffed. "Thankfully, Luke loves this place like I do."

He nodded. "Hopefully I can get us back into the black, financially. I don't want to see the property sold and broken up into subdivisions."

"That would break my heart," said Alice, the words wavering with emotion.

Silence spun out for a moment, and Callie's chest tightened as she realized what kind of pressure Luke must be under. No wonder he was concerned about Alice spending money they didn't have on something like a psychic. A thread of guilt twisted through her, and she reminded herself she hadn't taken any money yet. Nor would she, unless she actually managed to help. After all, she wasn't exactly flush with cash either.

She searched for something to say to bring the conversation back to practical grounds. "So are you going to...um, farm something again? Like, crops?" *God, she sounded idiotic.*

Luke chuckled, a deep, pleasant sound. "No, I think that ship has sailed for this property, at least in terms of growing and selling enough of anything that would turn a profit. We're going to board more horses, now that I'll be here to take care of them, and—"

Alice cleared her throat with exaggerated force.

He laughed again, reaching out to touch her shoulder. "Sorry. I meant, now that I'll be here to *help* Gram take care of the horses."

Walking slightly behind them, Callie smiled as they exchanged a look filled with quiet humor. But she sensed something else flowing between them—shared grief, an unspoken truth. The new reality of Henry's absence meant Alice simply couldn't manage the farm duties on her own, especially if they had more horses to care for. Not without Luke's living here.

His gaze traveled over the mostly empty fields. "I'm thinking we could get more of our own horses, too, and eventually offer trail rides for the tourists." He waved a hand at the expanse of woodlands fanning out from the fenced pastures. "Right now we only have six horses, and two of them are ours. We have room for a lot more in terms of acreage, and I'm going to add more stalls to the barn once I get my house finished."

The paved blacktop drive had given way to a dirt road once they'd passed the garage and started down the hill toward the barn, and Luke pointed out the remains of an older building under renovation, presumably the site of his eventual home. The sweet scent of freshly-cut lumber was replaced with the tang of hay and manure as they approached the barn.

A different cat—this one a gray tabby—glanced up at them from a sunny patch of packed dirt as they entered the barn. Inside, the air was still and cool, dust motes floating lazily through shafts of light. One enormous brown horse stood in its stall, although the back door leading to an enclosed pasture was wide open.

"This is Moose," said Luke, running his palm down the horse's mahogany neck. He scratched at the small white star between Moose's wide, half-closed eyes and added, "He's a homebody."

"Well, he's got a nice home," Alice pointed out. Opening her arms, she gestured to all the spacious stalls lining the center aisle. "Henry spent a lot of time in here. He found it peaceful." Alice turned and looked at Callie expectantly.

She didn't feel much, just a thrum of unease vibrating through her like a plucked sting. And there was a good chance that was more about the way the two of them were studying her now than a supernatural entity.

"It...is peaceful," she began, searching for the right words. It was true she didn't know how this so-called 'gift' worked, but when it had happened during her physical therapy sessions, it seemed like Karen's twin sister's spirit became stronger—and more demanding—with every encounter. "I can see why Henry liked to spend time in here," she continued, twining her fingers together. "But I don't feel anything right now."

To his credit, Luke kept his expression neutral, but disappointment pulled at Alice's features.

"Maybe if I spend more time here, and at the house." The words seemed to fall from Callie's lips of their own accord, and she drew in a breath as thoughts whirled through her mind. Was she crazy to even suggest that, given Luke's obvious disdain for her presence? *No.* This was about Alice. It was Alice who had sought her out, Alice she had agreed to try to help. And there was something going on here. The warning of danger *had* come through the way other messages had in the past. And something—or someone—*had* poked her in the back. She wasn't imagining things.

Recalling the painful jab, she suppressed a shudder. Nothing had ever touched her physically like that before. She wouldn't even *think* to imagine that.

Alice nodded enthusiastically, hope lighting in her eyes. "Yes, of course."

Before Luke could say anything, Callie blurted out, "I wouldn't accept any money, though, just for spending time here. I just want to see if I can help."

"We'd love that," Alice quickly insisted, a broad smile spreading across her face.

Callie wasn't so sure about the use of "we" in that proclamation, but Luke remained silent. *He must really care about his grandmother's happiness to put up with this.* She'd just figure out a way to avoid him while she was here. The property was certainly large enough to allow that.

"Oh, I have an idea!" Alice clapped her hands together, flicking her gaze between Luke and Callie. "Why don't the two of you go on a trail ride tomorrow? Callie said her schedule is pretty open right now, and Moose needs to get some exercise while his owner's away. Callie can ride one of our horses." Striding over to Moose's stall, she reached up to smooth his thick mane. "You can show her more of the land," she added, her tone growing slightly more forceful as she turned to face Luke.

Callie's mouth dropped open as she scrambled for a

polite way to release Luke from his grandmother's request. "Oh, no, that's okay. I don't really know how to ride. I was probably fifteen the last time I went." The memory of that family vacation flashed through her mind, accompanied by a dull ache in her chest. Her parents had both been alive and healthy. So much had changed in ten years. Swallowing hard, she touched the dragonfly pendant hanging from her neck.

Alice beamed. "Well, then, it's about time you got back in the saddle, so to speak. Our horses are pretty docile, and Luke's a good teacher."

She cleared her throat, twisting the necklace through her fingers. "I'm sure Luke doesn't really have time for that." Or the patience.

"Nonsense. You'd be doing us a favor. The horses need exercise, and I get tired easily these days. Plus, tomorrow's my baking day. The ladies and I have our weekly get together tomorrow afternoon."

She didn't believe for a second Alice often found herself too tired to ride a horse through the woods, if they were as docile as she claimed. Although Alice *had* injured her shoulder not too long ago, and she was still doing physical therapy with Karen, which was how she had found out about Callie's abilities. Still, the injury didn't seem to be preventing Alice from resuming her normal activities at this point. More likely, she just really wanted Callie to come to the farm tomorrow and spend more time searching for a connection to Henry, and the more plans that were set up, the less likely Callie might bow out with some invented excuse.

It had already become quite apparent, in just a few encounters, that Alice was more than ready to meet any challenge with unwavering persistence if she was determined to make something happen. There was steel beneath that soft, sweet exterior. What concerned Callie more was the tiny piece of herself that suddenly *wanted* to go. It made no sense. This man thought she was a scam artist; he didn't like or trust her. But there was something about him that tugged at her, a spark of chemistry humming through her veins. Surely one-sided, but she couldn't deny that she felt it. *Crazy.*

Alice stroked the horse's muzzle. "I think this boy needs a treat. I'll see if I can find a carrot." Turning, she strode past the ladder to the hayloft and disappeared down a hallway.

Pressing her lips together, Callie exhaled as she dragged her gaze back to Luke. "Sorry about that."

He shrugged. "No worries. It's just a pleasure ride." Adjusting his hat, he added, "The horses actually do need it, and you might even enjoy yourself."

"I'm sure I will," she replied quickly. "It's been a long time since I did anything for pleasure."

He gave her a long, appraising look, brows lifted. "Oh?" A few beats of silence spun out as something flashed in his eyes. The corners of his mouth twitched. "That's too bad."

Flames swept across her cheeks. *Oh, God.* Could she have turned his original phrase into a more embarrassing comment? Even if it *was* fairly accurate. Her throat went as dry as the sawdust and packed dirt beneath her feet, and she forced a noncommittal sound out as she made a

31

dismissive gesture with her hands that hopefully conveyed a casual 'oh, well, that's life' response. Seeking to hide her crimson face, she crossed the aisle back toward the wide entrance to the barn.

She stood in the middle of the doorway, folded her arms, and gazed out at the emerald fields. It really was beautiful here. Pulling in a deep breath, she willed her galloping pulse to slow down. *Get a hold of yourself.* It was just a silly slip-up...hilarious, really. But every nerve in her body had tingled as his gaze had raked over her, and she thought she'd sensed a hint of something deeper beneath his amusement...maybe a flicker of desire?

Ridiculous. It was probably just profound sympathy for her dull, pleasure-free life.

A sudden chill washed over her, and she glanced up, expecting to see a rogue dark cloud. But the sky was a clear, uninterrupted expanse of blue. A soft creak from directly above her head pulled her gaze higher, and she had a split second to register the pop of nails slipping from wood before an iron horseshoe hurtled down toward her upturned face.

Crying out, she lurched forward, stumbling as the metal U cracked against the back of her head. Pain ricocheted through her skull, turning her vision gray. She threw out a hand to break her fall, but her forward momentum came to an abrupt halt as strong arms caught her around the waist. She gasped, blinking at the ground, her dragonfly pendant swaying wildly as if ready to take flight. Her sunglasses, tossed from their perch on top of her head, lay in the gravel-studded dirt.

"Whoa." Luke hauled her up, turning her toward him while he kept one arm firmly wrapped around her back. His blue eyes blazed with concern as they locked with hers. "Are you okay?"

For a moment, all she could think about was the proximity of their bodies, pressed together in an intimate embrace. Then another shock of cold air swirled around her, clearing the haze in her mind and raising goosebumps along her skin.

His brow furrowed, as though he had also felt the strange chill, and his muscles tensed. He glanced around, still holding her close.

"Luke? Callie?" Alice's voice floated out from inside the barn.

They separated quickly, but Luke kept a steadying hand on the small of her back. "Out here, Gram," he called over his shoulder before turning back to her. "You okay?" he repeated under his breath.

She gave a shaky nod, heat rising in her cheeks once again. Lifting her hand, she touched the sore spot on the back of her head, wincing as her fingers encountered a sticky warmth. A crimson smear stained her fingertips, and she wiped the blood against her jeans.

Luke muttered a curse, steering her back toward the barn. "Let's get you sitting down."

"What's happened?" Alice's eyes grew wide as she came through the entrance, a bag of carrots dangling in her hand.

"Nothing." Callie pulled away from Luke's grasp, smoothing her hair.

"The old horseshoe fell and hit her on the head," said Luke, bending to pick it up off the ground. He plucked two nails from the dirt as well, staring at them for a moment.

"Oh, no! Are you all right?"

"I'm fine," she insisted, pasting a smile on her face. She was coming off as quite accident-prone today, and all the attention made her feel foolish. But had it been an accident? At least Luke had actually seen the horseshoe fall. He couldn't accuse her of inventing *that* for effect.

"No, she's not. She's bleeding." Luke closed his fist around the nails and glanced up at the spot where the horseshoe had hung as they crossed the threshold. "That thing's been up there forever," he said slowly, shaking his head.

Motioning them all toward a narrow bench in the aisle, Alice moved a plastic bucket filled with combs and brushes to the floor. "Have her sit down for a minute. I'll go get some ice." She hurried off back around the corner, still clutching the forgotten carrots.

Resigned, Callie lowered herself onto the bench. She really was fine, but she didn't have the energy to fight Alice's instructions at the moment.

Luke stared at the horseshoe in his hand for a few seconds before depositing it on a shelf. He returned, his tall form looming over her. Adjusting his hat, he cleared his throat. "I'm sorry that happened. You seem to be taking a beating today."

She lifted a shoulder. "It's no big deal. I'm tougher than I look."

"I'm beginning to see that."

Another pulse of desire fluttered through her, and she was grateful when Alice came rushing back, gripping a worn towel bulging with ice.

"It's not pretty, but it's clean," Alice said as she raised the ragged bundle. "Let me look at it first."

Callie bent forward, tipping her chin to her chest, allowing Alice to probe her scalp with gentle fingers.

"It's not too deep," Alice declared, settling the wrapped ice against the back of Callie's head. She stepped back as Callie took over holding the ice, a frown still deepening the lines around her mouth. "Do you feel dizzy? Maybe Luke should drive you home."

Mortified, Callie shook her head, inadvertently grinding the ice cubes against her wound. *Ow.* "Oh, no, that's not necessary. I'm really fine." She swallowed past the lump swelling in her throat. It had been quite some time since anyone had been concerned about her welfare. While it was sweet, it was unwarranted in this case. And something she shouldn't get used to. Thank God Alice didn't know about her past, or she'd be dialing an ambulance right now instead of standing next to Luke, staring down at her alongside her grandson. Callie was starting to feel like a bug under a microscope.

The sudden crunch of tires approaching had them all exchanging confused glances, and Luke returned to the doorway to peer out. "It's Mom."

Alice sighed, rolling her eyes.

"And Ryan." The engine cut off, and car doors opened and shut.

Alice brightened a bit. "That's my other grandson." She

35

hovered as Callie stood, seemingly ready to argue against this physical feat, but instead she just added, "He's Luke's younger brother. Only by a year, though."

They left the barn to join the others outside, and Callie glanced at the lumpy towel before hiding it behind her back. Only a small spot of blood. *Good.* She was more than ready to get out of here, especially with more family members arriving.

A tall woman with toned arms and frosted hair swept up in a chignon pulled away from Luke, leaving a trace of coral lipstick on his cheek. She wore a well-fitting skirt with a coordinated short-sleeved sweater set and low heels. "I called ahead," she said, a hint of annoyance lacing her tone, "but no one answered their phone."

"Like I said, we were all down here, and I forgot my ringer was off." Luke turned to Callie, reaching out to return her sunglasses. "Callie, this is my mother, Cynthia Turner. And my brother, Ryan."

Ryan was a less rugged, more polished version of Luke, with the same thick chestnut hair, strong jaw, and handsome features. But no dimples appeared around his mouth when he smiled at her, and his lips were thinner. "Nice to meet you," he said, echoing his mother.

Both Ryan and Cynthia studied her for a moment, bouncing questioning glances between the other members of the Turner family. Finally, Cynthia looked pointedly at Callie. "Are you a friend of Luke's, then?"

"Oh, no," Callie replied quickly, the seemingly permanent blush rising in her cheeks again. She realized her mistake, though, when she noticed the look of alarm passing over Alice's face. *Whoops.* Now how was she going to explain her presence here?

Inspiration hit. She waved her sunglasses in the direction of the barn before replacing them on top of her head. "I'm thinking of boarding my horse here."

Out of the corner of her eye, she caught Luke's barely concealed grin. He shot her a conspiratorial wink, and her stomach flipped.

"Oh, that's nice," said Cynthia, clearly losing interest. She nodded to her gold SUV. "I brought a bunch of leftovers from the charity luncheon. The caterers prepared some truly delicious dishes. I thought it would be helpful, especially with Luke here."

Callie could almost sense Alice gritting her teeth. Tension flowed between the two older women like a live current.

Luke jumped in. "Gram cooks great meals. And I have been known to survive on my own, if you remember." His words were nonchalant, his tone pleasant, but he looped a protective arm over Alice's shoulder.

"Well, there's no need for it to go to waste. I already gave some to Ryan, and it's too much for John and me."

Alice smiled brightly, patting Luke's hand. "Thank you, Cynthia, we appreciate it. Why don't you drive back up to the house, and we'll bring it in and put it away?"

Cynthia sniffed and nodded, walking back around to the driver's seat. "Does anyone want to ride up with me?"

"Callie, can we offer you a ride?" Ryan asked as he slid his hands into the pockets of his pressed khaki pants. His gaze traveled up and down her body before landing back on her face. "Or do you need some more time to look around? It would be great to have you here at Hillwood."

"We'll walk," Luke said firmly. "I can fill her in on the remaining details on the way. Why don't you two go ahead and start getting the stuff in the fridge?"

Yes. "That sounds perfect." She was more than ready to get back to her apartment, as quiet and lonely as it was. A dull ache had settled in the back of her head, and she needed some time to process the strange things that had happened here today. Besides, she was apparently coming back to the farm tomorrow. Her pulse skittered at the thought of a trail ride alone with Luke. What in the world had she gotten herself into?

Callie assured Alice and Luke she was feeling fine as they followed the SUV up the sloping drive, and she tossed the melting ice into the dirt, insisting on taking the old towel home to wash. Once she was alone in her car, she closed her eyes for a moment, massaging her temples. As she reached back to touch the tender lump forming on her scalp, another band of frigid air curled around her, and she froze. Her gaze shot to the dashboard temperature reading, but it remained unchanged. A shiver crept up her spine. Something strange was definitely going on at Hillwood Farm.

CHAPTER 5

*T*he lights began flickering just as she was getting out of the tub.

A late-night bath was her usual routine now, a way to unwind and relax after her workout. Most evenings, she taught either a Pilates or a Barre class from 6:15 to 7:30. It was a good way to supplement her income, and she received a free gym membership to boot. But most importantly, it got her out of her apartment after days spent mostly behind the computer screen, working as a freelance editor from home. After the accident, she'd begun avoiding situations that brought her around a lot of people—too many of them seemed to have restless spirits hovering around them, waiting for the opportunity to communicate. Her new abilities were like a beacon, flashing a welcoming light in the hazy realm between worlds.

But she'd found that while she was leading a class, as she'd done in college before the accident, her mind was too focused to let anything else in. Afterwards, she usually headed for a treadmill or bike in the farthest corner of the nearly empty gym to get her cardio in, headphones firmly in place.

A warm bath, a glass of wine, and a TV show or book would finish her night. It wasn't the most exciting life a 25-year-old could envision, but it was a life.

She paused as the bathroom lights blinked on and off sporadically, a towel pressed against her damp chest. A low crackle accompanied the flashes, and she frowned. That didn't sound good. With a sigh, she murmured, "Guess I need to change the bulbs," to the empty room. Living alone had her talking to herself more and more, just to break up the constant silence.

Steam filtered out as she opened the door and padded to her bedroom, wrapped in a towel. It was already after ten o'clock…she'd leave the bulb-changing chore till the morning. Hopefully there wasn't a wiring problem that would need the landlord's attention. The two-story building housing the 20 apartments wasn't exactly new.

Her room was small and dated, but she'd done her best to brighten it up with artwork and fabric. Pictures of sunflowers hung on the white walls, and blue and gold dragonflies danced across her fluffy comforter. A spider plant hung from the ceiling in the far corner, its green and white striped leaves trailing from the decorative pot. Tugging her fingers through her long wet hair, she crossed to the one set of windows and peered out into the night. A lone lamppost cast a cone of light onto the parking lot below; beyond the row of cars, a small clearing with picnic tables gave way to thick woods. She drew the pale yellow curtains partially closed, leaving the windows cracked to allow the cool air in.

Grabbing a comb off her dresser, she pulled it through her dark strands, careful to avoid the swollen lump on the back of her head. "I thought horseshoes were supposed to be lucky," she muttered, fighting with a tangle.

The lamp on her dresser flickered, and she froze, the hand holding the comb suspended in midair. So, the wiring then. Maybe it's about to go throughout the entire building. Great. Heaving out a heavy sigh, she adjusted the towel around her chest as she trudged over to the closet. The two sliding doors were paneled with mirrors, which served as a daily reminder of just how long it had been since this place was originally decorated. She slid one side open to peruse her wardrobe choices for tomorrow. "What am I supposed to wear on a trail ride with a hot guy?"

With a sharp pop, the light went out, plunging the room into darkness. Callie stilled, her heartbeat filling her ears. Something rustled behind her, and the hairs on her bare arms prickled. Probably a noise from outside, she told herself, blinking as her eyes adjusted to the trickle of faint light from the parking lot.

Another rustle, too close to pass off as wind in the trees. She was rooted in place, suddenly very sure she was not alone in the room. A soft moan floated through the blackness. Panic gripped her, fierce and primal, clawing at her lungs. Did she have a weapon? Would it even work against whatever was here?

She struggled for air, a rancid odor filling her nostrils as she slowly inhaled. Death. Decay. Shadows shifted to her left, and her gaze jerked toward the movement. Behind the solid mass of her reflection in the mirror, the gauzy outline of a face peered over her shoulder. Empty eye sockets stared out from gray, filmy features, the hollow black holes somehow filled with menace.

A sob gathered in her chest, clogging her throat. *Please, God. Let me wake up from this nightmare.* Something cold and wet brushed against her upper back, and she screamed.

The mirror exploded, shattering with a tremendous crack that reverberated through the silence. The horrific image disintegrated into fractured slivers as glass rained down onto the floor. She spun toward the door and fled from the room, her heart threatening to burst apart like the mirror. Pain flared up her leg as a jagged shard of glass pierced the ball of her foot, but she kept running until she slammed up against the front door, her chest heaving. She slapped at the light switch and miraculously, the room lit up. Still clutching the door knob, she searched the living area for signs of her ghoulish intruder.

No skeletal apparition pursued her from the bedroom. Her mind begged her to conclude the vision had been a figment of her imagination, but she knew that wasn't true. She hadn't imagined the mirror shattering—her throbbing foot was proof of that. No, there was something in this apartment, and it wasn't human.

Every cell in her body urged her to fling open the front door and run into the night, even in her current state of undress, with her bare feet leaking blood. *Just get away.* From that *thing.* But where would she go?

Her pulse thumped in her ears as she weighed her

options. It didn't take her long to realize there were none. Zero. She couldn't afford a hotel room in this tourist area, and even if she found a vacant room offering a reasonable rate, it would only solve the problem for one night. She could sleep in her car, maybe...but it would be cramped. And what was to stop the specter that had found her here from finding here there, curled in her small sedan, with nowhere to run?

Her predicament reminded her of all her losses, and her shoulders slumped as she leaned back against the door. Swallowing hard, she kept her eyes glued to the entrance to her bedroom, watching and waiting for what seemed like an eternity. Nothing materialized, and eventually the violent shudders wracking her body subsided to mild tremors.

If something like this had happened before she'd helped Karen communicate with her sister, she'd have already called 911. Lord knew she'd thought she was going crazy right after the accident, when she'd kept hearing Andrew's voice in her head, begging her not to blame herself. Wishful thinking, she'd thought at the time. But now she knew her abilities were real. Inexplicable, but genuine. Powerful.

It was just that she'd never actually *seen* a spirit. She'd imagined them flitting about, hovering over her as they whispered demands in her head...but this was a whole new experience. A terrifying one. Had it been Henry? If so, why would he smash her mirror? From all accounts, he'd been a kind, gentle man.

Perhaps tonight's incident was completely unrelated.

But that was a tough leap to make, considering she'd been poked in the back and pelted with a horseshoe earlier the very same day.

In her gut, she knew it was connected. Something—someone—had followed her home from Hillwood Farm. And it seemed intent on scaring her, if not outright harming her. Worst of all, there was no one who could help her with something like this. It was up to her to figure out what was going on, and hopefully put this malevolent spirit to rest.

Pulling in a deep breath, she pushed away from the door and rewrapped the towel around her chest. She crept toward her bedroom, doing her best to avoid putting weight on the ball of her right foot. Her eyes remained laser focused on the bedroom doorway as she paused by the kitchen counter and snagged a towel off the tall stool. The same towel she'd brought home from the farm today that she'd planned to wash tomorrow before she returned. What difference would a little more blood make? A bubble of hysterical laughter rose in her throat, but she swallowed it back down. *Hold it together.* She quickly swiped at her cut, hoping no glass remained embedded in her flesh. There'd be time to clean and examine it later. Assuming she survived till then.

Keeping her gaze glued on the door, she retrieved a flashlight from a drawer and drew a knife from the knife block, which made little sense but still felt right. Thankfully, the hall light clicked on when she tried the switch, and she ventured into the doorway of her room, sweeping the darkness with the beam of her flashlight.

Empty. Or, at least, no visible ghosts. A shiver bolted up her spine as hundreds of mirrored slivers glittered beneath the beam of light. *What a disaster.* How was she ever going to clean that up? She'd be charged for the damage, too.

The fact that practical thoughts were surfacing after the tidal wave of terror made her feel more in control. She could handle this. She had to. Still, there'd be no sleeping in here tonight, that was for sure. With a sigh, she looked longingly at her comfy bed before shutting the door to her bedroom firmly.

She quickly cleaned her cut in the bathroom, then brought her flashlight and her knife with her to the couch. Overhead lights still blazing, she curled up with a blanket and the television remote and settled in for a long night.

CHAPTER 6

*L*uke fought to remain focused on the piece of wood he was cutting, because being distracted while using a table saw was a bad idea. But he was agitated. Slightly off-kilter, as though there was a problem he needed to address, but he just couldn't remember what it was.

Callie.

He frowned, pulling the board off the table. She was coming back over for a trail ride this afternoon, and while he hated to admit it, he couldn't stop thinking about her. Or the conversation he'd had with his brother yesterday.

He and Ryan had lounged on the porch for a few minutes after all the caterer's trays were inside and Gram and Mom were dividing portions into plastic containers. Ryan leaned back in one of the wooden Adirondack chairs, taking a pull from an amber beer bottle.

"Happy Hour already?" Luke asked, raising his eyebrows.

Ryan shrugged. "It's 5:00 somewhere. I don't really need to go back to the office today." He tipped the bottle in Luke's direction. "Why don't you join me? Being your own boss is almost as good as having Dad as a boss."

He shook his head. "I still have a ton of work to do. I need to take care of the horses. Plus, I'm building a house, remember?"

"Yeah, yeah." Ryan rolled his eyes, but a grin twitched at his lips. "I could build a house if I wanted to."

"Sure you could. Probably about as well as I could practice law." They shared a laugh, gazing out over the sloping hills that hid all signs of the main road connected to Hillwood's long, winding driveway. A group of turkeys gathered in a field by the edge of the woods, the male fanning his tail, protecting his flock. Overhead, an osprey soared, making its way to the pond.

After a few moments, Ryan broke the silence. "So. That chick Callie is hot. You think she'll board her horse here?"

Doubtful, Luke thought to himself, suppressing a smile. "I don't know," he answered out loud. *Maybe she'll board her imaginary horse here while she hunts for our Pop's imaginary ghost.* Even as the silent sarcasm rolled through his mind, a tiny spark of satisfaction glowed at the memory of the moment he'd shared with Callie down at the barn earlier, when she'd so quickly come up with a cover story. She was clever and quick on her feet, in addition to being attractive. *Probably necessary traits for a scam artist*, he reminded himself. Still, he couldn't deny the heat he'd felt when he held her close, the arousal ignited by her body's proximity to his.

"Well, it wouldn't be a hardship to have her around here on a regular basis. Is she single?"

Luke tensed. "No idea."

"Seriously? You are clearly off your game. That would have been the first thing I'd have tried to find out."

"Yeah, well...after everything that happened over the winter, I'm not exactly looking for relationships."

Ryan let out a strangled groan. "That again? Seriously, Luke, you need to let that disaster go. Besides, getting some from a hot girl doesn't necessarily need to lead to a relationship."

It was a valid statement, something he agreed with. And yet, irritation bristled in his chest. "I'll let her know if she comes back again."

Ryan chuckled. "No-strings-attached sex with one of the Turner men would certainly be a selling point, don't you think? If she's on the fence about Hillwood." Swallowing a sip of beer, he waved his free hand inward, up and down the length of his chest. "Hopefully she makes the right choice."

Luke's muscles tightened, his fingers curling into an involuntary fist. He had a sudden, intense urge to punch his brother, which made no sense. Ryan was just joking around. At least for the most part. And so what if Ryan did want to sleep with Callie? If she was single and willing, it was none of his business.

So why did the thought of them together make his blood simmer? Even now, as he lined up the next board with the saw's blade, he ground his teeth together at the idea. *God.* Could he actually be falling for the woman who was probably hoping to con his grandmother out of her money?

Even if Callie was legit, he had no interest in romantic entanglements after his last train wreck of a relationship.

Blowing out a breath, he wiped the sweat beading at his hairline with his forearm. As he chugged from a nearby water bottle, he pulled his phone from his pocket and checked the time. Almost noon. Callie was due over at 2:00 for the trail ride. He capped the bottle and surveyed the morning's progress. Not bad. He'd get a little more done; then he could break for a shower and lunch. Afterwards, he'd get down to the barn to start tacking up the horses for his ride with Callie.

Her image flashed in his mind—the long, sable brown hair that shone with copper streaks. Clear green eyes, full pink lips, and smooth skin dusted with the faintest hint of freckles across the bridge of her nose. She *was* gorgeous. He'd noticed her scent, too, when he'd held her in his arms...her perfume had reminded him of green apples. And her body was strong and lean, with curves in all the right places.

His own body stirred as he thought about her pressed against him yesterday, and he shook his head to clear it. *Enough.* He had work to do, and losing a finger to the saw's blade would definitely be a detriment to his plans to help Gram. And to save Hillwood.

Rolling his shoulders back, he returned to his task.

ALICE HUMMED to herself as she sprinkled flour across the countertop, preparing to roll out the pie crusts. For at least twenty years now, Thursdays had been her baking day. There was something infinitely soothing about the routine, even though making pies from scratch could be fairly labor-intensive. But along with all the work came the anticipation of her weekly dinner with the ladies. Every Thursday evening, Alice and her friends—both old and new—gathered at one of their houses for a potluck meal, conversation and catching up, and of course, dessert. Alice always brought one of her famous pies, although she varied the fillings. Today she was making two cherry pies—one for this evening's dinner, one to have here at the farm for her and Luke.

Henry had loved her pies. A wave of grief washed over her as she spread the flour out with her palm. Now, more than ever, she valued the support of her friends, but oh, how she missed her husband. "I miss you," she whispered into the air, blinking back the sting of tears.

Her breath caught as cold air drifted around her, and she closed her eyes, frozen in place. Had he heard her? Was he here? The thud of her pulse filled her ears as she waited for something to happen, hope warring with fear in a fierce, potent clash of emotions.

A feathery touch grew in pressure as phantom arms encircled her from behind in a gentle hug. She longed to lean back into the comforting embrace, to savor the moment even as shivers raced up and down her spine. But the sensation lasted so briefly, she almost convinced herself she'd imagined it. Then she caught the faint scent of

Henry's spicy aftershave, and knew without a doubt that somehow, his presence was with her.

As if to further prove it, a shaky line began to form in the dusting of flour spread across the counter. Her mouth dropped open as she stared. An invisible finger parted the white powder, extending the vertical line downward.

Henry was trying to send her a message! She inhaled sharply, her mind reeling. The letter 'I'? Maybe he was trying to spell out 'I'm here'? 'I love you'?

But it wasn't an 'I', because more of the letter began to appear, a semicircle curving out from the top of the straight line. The kitchen lights flickered as she watched in fascination, and the preheating oven clicked off briefly, leaving the clock numbers flashing.

A loop began to close as the curve came back in toward the middle of the straight line. In the moment before the semicircle connected, the temperature in the kitchen dropped, and time stood still. Suddenly, flour burst into the air in a violent snowstorm, as if an unseen hand had swept across the counter. The fledgling message disappeared in the fury, and Alice cried out. The bowl of pitted cherries smashed to the floor, splattering crimson juice and ceramic shards across the wooden planks. Round red globes rolled in every direction.

She spun in a circle, looking for the cause of the chaos. But of course, there was no one there. No one visible, anyway. Wrapping her arms around her chest, she released a small sob. She was more distraught over the loss of the message, of the connection to Henry, than her morning's hard work, but now she was facing a big clean-up job as well.

She took a few wobbly steps over to the big table in the dining room and lowered herself into the chair on the end. Henry's chair. Leaning back, she lifted her gaze to the ceiling, as though he might be hovering above, ready to offer an explanation.

Because there had to be one. None of this made sense. Why would Henry offer her a comforting hug and begin a message, only to wipe it away unfinished in a furious tantrum? Why would he smash her bowl of cherries, or the sugar bowl, for that matter?

The thread of an idea wound its way into her chaotic thoughts, and she tugged at it, unraveling, considering. Maybe it fit. Pulling in a determined breath, she pushed herself up and picked her way through the kitchen, in search of her cell phone. When she located it by the sink, she pulled up Callie's number and made the call.

CHAPTER 7

*C*allie's hands tightened around the steering wheel as she turned into Hillwood's long driveway. She'd rushed to get ready when Alice had called and told her there'd been an incident, and asked if she could come over sooner than the 2:00 p.m. arrival originally planned for the trail ride. Alice hadn't elaborated on the phone, but after everything that had happened in the apartment last night, Callie was dreading whatever was coming. Licking her lips, she turned off her music and pulled over to the parking area to the left of the house.

A twinge of pain throbbed in the ball of her foot as she stepped out of the car, and she winced. It was bearable, though, and she'd bandaged the sliced skin carefully. She knew enough about horseback riding to know that the stirrup wouldn't put a lot of pressure on the injured area of her foot. Teaching an hour class standing in front of a ballet barre was a different story, though. Luckily, tonight was Pilates, and she could do everything sitting or lying on a mat. There were no classes on Friday nights, so she could have the rest of the weekend to heal up.

Provided there were no more wild events at her apartment, that was. Unfortunately, Alice's call didn't give her much hope that things were calming down. If anything, the situation was escalating, quickly.

Climbing the porch steps, she smoothed her hair back and closed her eyes for a brief moment, struggling to center herself. Then she tapped on the screen door frame and stepped inside when Alice's "come in" called out from the kitchen.

A word slammed into her head: *Help*. Then garbled sounds took over, underscored with static, as though a radio station had suddenly veered beyond the range of its signal. A bright ache bloomed in her skull, and she gasped, lifting her hand to her forehead as if she could physically calm the chaos roiling inside. "Whoa," she gasped, swaying.

Alice rushed toward her, gripping her arm. "Did you hear something?"

She hesitated, straining to hear something else intelligible beneath the crackling in her head. Nothing. The din began to fade away, and she opened her eyes and shrugged. "Sort of," she hedged as she followed Alice through the dining room and into the kitchen. She wanted to find out what had happened here first before she went into all the details of her experiences.

A mop and bucket stood in the corner. Uh oh. That didn't bode well. Her mind flashed back to the millions of tiny glass shards glittering all over the worn carpet of her bedroom. She'd spent over an hour trying to pick up the larger pieces, then vacuuming over and over, the whole time warily looking over her shoulder for a gauzy, terrifying face. And this after a night spent on the couch, drifting in and out of a splintered sleep. At least nothing else had happened since the mirror incident. Well, to her, anyway.

"More destruction?"

Alice nodded, folding her hands across her chest. "A big bowl of cherries I'd already pitted smashed onto the floor. And flour went everywhere too. But before all that, something else very strange happened." With a sigh, she gestured toward the row of stools beneath the counter where Callie had sat yesterday. "Do you want to sit down? Can I get you anything?"

"I'm fine, thanks." She slid onto a stool. "Tell me what happened."

"I was getting ready to roll out the pie crusts, and I said how much I missed Henry out loud." Her voice broke, and she pulled in a shaky breath. "And then I felt him here. Like a presence, but it was like he was standing behind me, and wrapped his arms around me. I *felt* it. And then..." She paused, exhaled. "A message started forming in the flour. Like, a letter. But then it was suddenly swept away. And the bowl went crashing down."

"A letter?" Wow. This was huge. "What was it?"

"It looked like the letter 'P'. But it was erased before any more was written." She shook her head, frowning. "It was just like what happened with the sugar bowl. The atmosphere went from loving and gentle to angry and destructive. I just don't understand. But I have an idea I wanted to talk to you about. First, though, did you hear something when you came in?"

Reaching back, Callie massaged the knot in her neck. Sleeping on the couch had not done her body any favors. "Um...I did. But I should start by telling you I heard something yesterday, too." She bit her lip as a wave of guilt washed over her. "I just wanted to wait to mention it, so I could get more context. But I'm as stumped as ever." She relayed the danger message, along with today's plea for help, finishing with last night's fiasco at her apartment.

"Oh, Callie, I am so sorry that happened to you!" Alice's pale blue eyes went wide, filling with concern. The corners of her mouth sank as she wrapped an arm around Callie's shoulders. "This is my fault. I got you involved. I never dreamed something would happen away from Hillwood." The words quaked with emotion.

"Please don't feel bad, Alice. I didn't think of it either. Nothing this...aggressive...has ever happened to me. Usually, the spirits that try to communicate with me are just looking for help. It's frightening, or at least it was when it first began happening, but it's never felt dangerous before." She pulled her brows together. "There are those two words again. Danger and help. I just don't get why there seems to be so much...interference. The messages being drowned out by other noises. The letter in the flour being wiped away. It's like any attempts at communication are getting cut off somehow."

Alice nodded emphatically, sliding onto an empty stool. "That goes along with my theory." She pinned Callie with a steady gaze. "I don't think this is just Henry. I think

Henry's trying to tell me something." Her voice dropped. "And someone is trying to stop him."

Oh my God. Callie's jaw dropped open. It made sense. "That would explain...a lot," she said slowly. "But who? And why?"

"I haven't been able to come up with any answers to those questions yet. If it's true, it's a lot to take in."

"Yes." Her own mind was whirling like one of the carnival rides at the Barnstable County Fair. "Could it be someone with a name that begins with 'P'?"

Alice propped her elbows on the counter and settled her forehead on her fists. "I've been wracking my tired, old brain for the last hour. I can't think of anyone who might have lived here or spent a lot of time here whose name begins with 'P'."

"Well, 'P' could be the person trying to block Henry's message. Or the person Henry's trying to warn us about. Or both." Her shoulders slumped as frustration combined with exhaustion. This was maddening.

"Or maybe it was the start of a different word. Like...'Please'?"

"Hmm. Where was it written, exactly?"

Alice traced her finger across the surface of the counter with slow strokes.

Callie chewed in the inside of her cheek, following the path of Alice's fingertip. "Or...maybe it wasn't even a 'P'. It could have been an unfinished 'R'."

Their eyes met. *Ryan?* The silent suggestion passed between them. Alice pursed her lips, deepening the network of tiny wrinkles, and shook her head.

Boots thumped on the porch steps, and the screen door opened with a whine. Alice and Callie snapped their heads toward the front hall.

Luke walked in, bare-chested, toweling the perspiration from the back of his neck with his T-shirt. He stopped in his tracks as he noticed Callie sitting beside Alice. "Oh."

Muscles rippled across the hard planes of his chest, the wide V of his shoulders tapering down to washboard abs. A heady thrill traveled through her, hot and demanding. She gulped, dragging her gaze away as she willed the flush rising in her cheeks to recede.

He took a few steps toward the dining area, his eyes sliding to the large white clock on the wall. His brows furrowed. "I thought…"

"I asked Callie to come over early," explained Alice.

"Ah. Well, I was just going to grab a shower." He glanced down at his upper body, then gestured with the hand clutching the damp T-shirt. "It's really humid out there."

"Yes," Callie agreed, struggling to yank a coherent thought from the current haze in her brain. Nothing came, but she managed to resist the urge to echo "it *is* really humid". Although it really was, unfortunately. Her skin felt sticky, her hair heavy and weighed down. She'd given up this morning and wrapped it into a knot on the top of her head, being careful to avoid the painful lump.

He narrowed his eyes. "Wait. Is there something I need to know about?"

Alice waved him away. "It can wait. Go ahead and take your shower. We're fine. We can discuss it after."

He looked at Callie, clearly seeking confirmation that all was well.

She nodded. "Everything's fine, really." *Please, go shower and put some clothes on. For the love of God.*

"I won't be long," he said as he turned and disappeared up the stairs.

Callie blinked to clear the image of his broad back from her brain. Focus. There were more important things at stake here than her sudden overwhelming lust for Luke. Like how they were going to explain all this to him, for one thing. Keeping her voice low, she leaned in toward Alice. "Do you think he'll believe us?"

Alice lifted a narrow shoulder, sighing. "He'll believe the mishaps happened, and maybe that I saw a letter in the flour. But he'll look for a rational explanation, probably." She offered an apologetic smile. "He doesn't mean anything by it."

"I know. It's a difficult thing to accept."

"He's a good man. Special."

That was one word to describe him, she thought to herself, trying not to picture him upstairs in the shower. A few others that came to mind were hot, kind, protective, loyal, funny, and hardworking. Able to build a house. A freaking cowboy, or as close to one as you would find on Cape Cod. She wondered idly if he had a girlfriend. Of course he did. Women were probably lining up to date him. Ugh. And why was she thinking about this? "I can tell," she managed, when she noticed Alice seemed to be waiting for a reply.

A knowing look gleamed in Alice's eyes, and one corner of her mouth quirked up.

Oh, God. She'd been caught—apparently it wasn't too difficult for the older woman to read Callie's thoughts. About her grandson, for God's sake. Callie dropped her chin to hide her face, pretending to tighten the band securing her thick coil of hair. Then she added, "I can't imagine how he's going to react when we try to convince him there might be two ghosts lurking about."

"If that's indeed the case," said Alice, "which one do you think is speaking to you? Can you tell anything from the voice?" She drummed her fingers lightly against the counter as she thought for a moment. "What about the face you saw? I know you said it was dark, but did you notice anything that might help us figure out who this is? Male, female, old, young?"

"Hmm. Well, each time I've heard a voice, it's been a single word, and it sounds like it's coming from far away. Like a whisper traveling through a bad phone connection. It's a lot less clear than some of the other times I've heard messages. Plus, it's like it's being purposefully garbled. I'd just assumed the voice belonged to Henry, since he lived here so long and passed away so recently. But I can't be certain it's a male voice, to be honest." She glanced up at the ceiling, trying to replay the messages in her head.

"And the face was…" she trailed off, suppressing a shudder. She swallowed, tried again. "The face seemed like it was made of smoke and shadows. The room was dark, like you said, and I was terrified. But I noticed dark, empty sockets where eyes should be, and blurry features. I suppose it could have been my imagination, but then I felt something touch me, and the mirror exploded."

"I don't think for one minute you imagined it." Alice gave her thigh a comforting pat, then stood and walked around the counter to the sink. She took two glasses from a cabinet, filling them with ice and water at the fridge door.

"I'm certain I didn't. It wasn't even something I'd thought of, that might have been lodged in my subconscious, since I've never actually seen a ghost. I've only heard them."

With a heavy sigh, Alice set the water glass in front of her. "I am so sorry this is happening to you, Callie. I wouldn't have asked for your help if I'd had any idea the haunting would...follow you home."

"It never occurred to me, either," she said, taking a drink. "The only time spirits have ever communicated with me when I'm alone is when it's been someone attached to me. Someone I actually knew." Like Mom. Like Andrew. Her heart twisted into a painful knot.

Footsteps jogged down the stairs, and Luke appeared, this time fully dressed in worn jeans and a white T-shirt, his hair still damp. He slid onto the stool next to Callie. "Okay ladies, fill me in."

CHAPTER 8

*A*lice made sandwiches while they talked, and after lunch, Luke asked Callie if she was still up for a trail ride. A few butterflies skittered through her stomach as she assured him she was. Alice was still determined to get at least one pie made, so she shooed them out of the kitchen with instructions to have fun.

"I'll ride Moose," Luke said as they walked down to the barn. "He can be very stubborn, and he'll try to turn around to get back to the barn. I was going to have you ride Lady."

"Well, the name sounds promising, anyway. A horse named Lady wouldn't run away with me, right?"

He chuckled. "She's very gentle. And we'll just keep it at a walk. I'll go over all the basic stuff you need to know, but for the most part, it's likely she'll just follow Moose."

When they got to the barn, she watched him saddle the horses, being careful to avoid standing under anything that might tumble from above and strike her on the head. Her nerves were humming, and she was having difficulty pinpointing exactly what was making her more anxious: the unfamiliarity of riding a horse, the awkward intimacy of being alone with Luke, or the very real possibility of another hostile paranormal event. All three were probably equally to blame, she decided, glancing up at the ceiling.

Thankfully, Luke seemed to have lost some of the antagonism he displayed toward her yesterday. While he didn't exactly say he believed they were being haunted, he listened patiently and asked thoughtful questions. Like Alice had predicted, he clearly felt there was some rational explanation for everything that had happened, but he didn't accuse Callie of making things up for monetary gain. He also didn't suggest anyone was going crazy, which was an unexpected vote of confidence.

When he'd finished tacking up the horses, he tipped his chin toward the entrance to the barn. "Ready?" He left Moose in the aisle cross-ties and led Lady outside by the reins.

Lady was a beautiful gray mare, with a silvery dappled coat and a white mane and tail. She seemed sweet, too, but Callie's pulse ramped up a little as she prepared to mount. Did the horse get taller since they'd left the barn?

Luke tugged on the metal stirrup. "You put your left foot in here, hold onto the front and back of the saddle, and swing your right leg over as you pull yourself up." He glanced between her and Lady, gauging their relative heights. "I can give you a leg up," he added, lacing his fingers.

Her pride shoved its way past any jitters. "No, it's fine, I can do it." Thank goodness she'd worn loose jeans, belted low around her waist and cuffed at the ankles. She brought her knee up high enough to slide a low-heeled boot into the stirrup, gripped the ends of the saddle, and hoisted herself up in one fairly smooth movement.

His brows shot up. "Wow. You made that look easy. Push your heels down," he added, checking the stirrup length.

"Well, I teach fitness classes four nights a week. Pilates and Barre."

"Yeah?" He glanced up at her, his gaze lingering. "It shows." Stepping back, he nodded at her position on the horse. "You're all set. Don't move, I'll be right back."

"You hear that, Lady?" she murmured, and the horse's ears flicked backward. She stroked her soft neck, replaying Luke's words as he disappeared into the barn. What did he mean by 'it shows'? Just that she was able to get herself into the saddle without help? Or was he referring to the fact that she stayed in shape? Either way, she would take it as a compliment. A tiny bud of happiness bloomed in her chest, and she smiled to herself.

She stayed fit and active for her own health—both mental and physical—not to catch the attention of men. Even if that were her goal, it would be pointless. She was never going to be in a normal relationship; she couldn't even go to public places without risking being hounded by desperate spirits. Still, it was nice to have the strenuous regimen she put her body through acknowledged.

Especially by Luke, her inner voice whispered, and she bit down hard on her lip to silence it. The truth was that he was probably still a bit suspicious of her, despite being too polite to mention it again. Plus, there was that girlfriend thing…maybe she just needed to get confirmation that he was taken, so she could shut down her inappropriate thoughts, once and for all.

Luke returned, leading Moose, and he swung himself easily into the saddle. "Ready?" he asked, circling the horse around until he was beside Callie.

"Ready."

"We'll go this way, along the outside of the fence toward the pond." He transferred the reins to one hand and pointed toward a worn path through the grass which led back into the woods. In the distance, to the right of the water, a break in the tree line revealed the entrance to the trail.

As Luke nudged Moose's flank with his heels and guided the horse away from the barn, Lady followed automatically. Callie's legs relaxed slightly from their death grip around the saddle once Lady settled into a leisurely walk, and she found herself enjoying the view rather than worrying about falling off.

Luke was in front of her, clearly at ease in the saddle, the muscles of his back and arms stretching the fabric of the white T-shirt, the gold streaks in his hair glinting in the sunlight. To her right, a white split-rail fence enclosed one of the pastures, with access to the back of the barn; on the left, the dark blue-green water of the lake shimmered as insects buzzed over the surface.

Luke moved slightly off of the path, allowing Callie and Lady to come up alongside him and Moose. "All okay?"

"Perfect. This is great, actually. Thank you for taking me." She'd almost said 'inviting me', but that hadn't exactly been the case.

"So, you're a Pilates teacher? And..." He trailed off, shooting her a questioning look as he searched for the other word she'd used.

"And Barre. It's like a workout using a ballet barre. A lot of squats and leg lifts," she added. "Sometimes I fill in and teach Yoga classes too, although technically I'm not certified to do that."

He gave her a sideways grin. "So you're a rule-breaker."

She laughed. "I suppose, in some small way. I consider it helping out, and any classes I can teach help pay the bills. Although my main source of income comes from my other job. I majored in English, and I do freelance editing from home. But it's sporadic. Sometimes I'm overwhelmed with projects, and sometimes there's no business at all."

"And in your spare time you're a ghost whisperer?"

She chuckled again, although a thread of tension snaked through her. "Something like that. Although like I told you, I don't advertise that, and I have never accepted money for it."

"Until now."

Her grip on the reins tightened. "Maybe. We'll see." This was not a topic she wanted to revisit right now. Not when they had been having a nice conversation, laughing together. She pulled in a deep breath, savoring the sweet, warm scent of the horses, the marshy tang of the lake, and the crisp pine of the woods. "What do you do?" she asked, hoping to steer the conversation away from psychic abilities and dueling spirits.

"Well, right now I'm in the business of saving the farm." He cleared his throat, sweeping his gaze over the property. "But I'm a carpenter by trade. A Certified Lead Carpenter, technically. I have an associate's degree in business as well, and I owned a construction company for a few years. I sold it not too long ago."

"Wow." That explained why he was able to build a house and renovate the barn on his own. "That's impressive."

He shrugged. "Not really. My dad pushed for law school, but it wasn't for me." He was quiet for a moment, only the soft plod of the horses' hooves breaking the silence. "But he's got Ryan working with him, and he can take over the practice someday. I'll do this." He waved a hand in an arc over the fields to their right.

"It's a big job to take on. But an important one. I'm sure it's stressful for you."

"The Turner family established Hillwood Farm, and I'm not going to let our generation be the one to lose it." His words rang with quiet determination.

"I realize I don't know you very well, but you seem like the kind of person who succeeds at what he sets his mind to." It occurred to her that she wasn't just saying this to be supportive; she truly believed it. This was a man who'd followed his passion, despite pressure from his family. Created a successful business and sold it. Moved in with his grandmother when she'd lost her husband and begun building his own home on the property. "If I had to bet, I'd bet on you," she added, admiration for him swelling in her chest.

They returned to single file as they entered the woods, and for a while it was just the chattering of birds and squirrels in the trees, the crunch of dried leaves and forest detritus beneath the horses' hooves, and the rustle of small animals in the tangled undergrowth. Sunlight filtered in through the branches overhead, and the shade from the arching boughs offered relief from the humidity. The air was still and warm, but in this peaceful sanctuary, it felt magical instead of oppressive.

Every once and a while, Luke would point out something of interest—a red-tailed hawk soaring overhead, the remains of an old hunting cabin, a low stone wall covered in pale green lichen, an old fort built by Luke and Ryan in the branches of a tree. Eventually, the trail opened up to a clearing, with a meandering stream snaking through it. The horses approached eagerly and lowered their heads to the water.

"Let up on the reins so they can slide up her neck," Luke instructed.

She copied Luke's example, combing her fingers through Lady's coarse mane as she drank. Downstream, a large dead branch had become lodged along the bank, and leaves and small sticks collected in the makeshift dam.

"This is so relaxing," she said, glancing up at the sky. A few wispy clouds stretched across the endless blue like torn lace. "I'm so glad I came."

"Me too," he said, his voice low.

"Really?" The words slipped out before she could corral

them. But she truly was surprised to hear that. She held his gaze for an intense moment as she waited for his response.

"Yes. We should do this again. Bring Sasha next time."

Her heart sank, punctured by an unexpected stab of jealousy. Sasha? Still, this was the opening she'd been waiting for. She took it. "Is that your girlfriend?"

Confusion clouded his features for a beat before mirth broke through, and his laughter rang through the woods. "No," he said, swallowing back another chuckle. "Sasha is our other horse. I don't have a girlfriend." He shook his head, wiping at his eyes. "Sorry. I don't know why I found that so funny."

She giggled too, giddy with relief. "No, I'm sorry. I guess I just assumed."

"No worries." He cleared his throat, reaching around to rub the back of his neck. "What about you?"

It took her a second to realize what he was asking: did she have a boyfriend? Of course, she should have seen that coming, since she'd asked his status. Then again, she couldn't really imagine a scenario where he actually cared. Just because she'd felt sparks of chemistry between them didn't mean he did. And even if he did, it didn't necessarily mean anything beyond an instinctive physical reaction to the opposite sex.

She felt his eyes on her, and she realized he was still waiting for a response.

"No boyfriend," she said. But that felt wrong. Like a betrayal to Andrew. "There was someone," she added. "Now there's not."

He gave a small nod. "Yeah, that's pretty much my story."

She inhaled sharply. *What?* Then she realized he didn't know her story, and he probably assumed she was referring to a break-up. That's what he meant. But that was not her story.

Every time she thought of Andrew, guilt and sadness engulfed her until she thought she might drown, despite the messages he'd fought so desperately to send. Already, she could feel the ragged hole in her heart opening up, and more than anything, she wanted to avoid discussing the subject of significant others any further. So far, the trail ride had been amazing, and right now, she wanted to live in the present—appreciate the sounds and scents of nature around them, the conversation with the man beside her, the soothing presence of the horse below her.

"This trail is a big circle, we're just about halfway around the loop. Ready?" He pulled on the reins and made a clicking sound, turning Moose's head back toward the path.

Phew. Apparently Luke didn't want to talk about the past either. And who would, really? She didn't have much experience with relationships beyond Andrew, but most people probably didn't relish chatting about their break-ups.

Forty minutes later, they were headed back to the barn, and the filmy clouds were coalescing into a darker mass in the distance. "Looks like we're getting back just in time," Callie said, although truthfully, she didn't want their time together to end. She'd loved learning about Luke and

Ryan's childhood antics here on the farm, and all the fun they'd had roaming the property with little supervision. Apparently their mother hadn't known exactly what they were up to, but she'd been happy to let the two boys spend weekends and summers at Hillwood, getting dirty and expending their energy somewhere besides the elegant, orderly house Cynthia liked to decorate with expensive fabrics and valuable art.

In comparison, her own childhood seemed a lot less rambunctious; she was an only child who spent a great deal of time with her nose in a book. But she'd had her own wonderful world of adventures in her imagination—and in the magical kingdom she and her father had created.

It was the one detail from her past she'd shared with Luke today—how, when she was a little girl, she'd loved to play in their backyard garden, and she'd become entranced by the jewel-colored dragonflies that hovered over the little koi pond.

Her father had been a creative writing teacher at the local high school, and he began making up fairy tales revolving around Princess Callie and the Dragonfly Kingdom. Together, they developed an increasingly elaborate fictional world, with all sorts of magic and mayhem. Eventually, Thomas Sinclair typed up the scenes, Callie and her mother made the illustrations, and they had a set of books. To this day, she still had them all, and the dragonfly necklace her father had given her for her thirteenth birthday.

She reached for the pendant now, sliding her thumb over the tiny crystal eyes. Lady came to a stop near the barn entrance as Luke reined Moose to a halt in front of them.

He dismounted, turning toward her. "Did you want to stick around for a while? Once I get the horses untacked, we can go up to the house and see if there's some pie we can swipe. You haven't lived till you've tasted Gram's pie," he added with a grin.

Her pulse surged—he actually wanted her to stick around. She opened her mouth to reply, but the words caught as a chill curled around her. Lady sidestepped nervously, and Callie had a split second to wonder if the inexplicable cold air was a result of the dark clouds gathering to the west. Then a sharp hiss sliced through her head, a cross between a high-pitched screech and fingernails dragging across a blackboard. Her temples throbbed with the sound, and Lady suddenly reared up as though something terrifying had scuttled in front of her.

Lady's neck hit her chest, the impact pitching Callie back in the saddle. All her muscles tightened, her legs clamping around the saddle like a vise, her fingers yanking at Lady's mane. Somehow, she stayed on, even as she cried out in surprise and fear.

Cursing loudly, Luke dropped Moose's reins and rushed over, grabbing Lady's bridle. "Shh," he murmured, calming her. He held the horse steady, sliding his free hand along her neck, then placing it over Callie's fist with a gentle squeeze. "You okay?"

Was she? Her heart slammed against her ribcage, and fresh sweat dampened her already sticky skin. But she was okay. She nodded, wanting to reassure him as much as herself.

She was no worse for the wear, this time. But she'd been targeted—again.

"Something must have spooked her," Luke said, checking their surroundings.

Hysterical laughter bubbled in her chest at his choice of words, but she pushed it back down. She wasn't going to ruin the pleasant afternoon they'd had by bringing up hostile ghosts again. Although something about the way he was looking at her made her think he had his own unspoken suspicions.

"Let's get you down," he said. Taking the reins from her shaking grip, he added, "Just swing your leg over in the reverse of how you got on. I've got you."

Her pride rose up, ready to insist she didn't need help. But her legs were still trembling, and the muscles that had served her so well up to this point were starting to feel weak. It wouldn't be a good look to collapse on the ground, and then his hands settled around her waist, and his touch was suddenly all she could focus on.

His grip was firm as he helped her down, and when both her feet were on the ground, he turned her to face him. She was sandwiched between the horse's side and Luke, and he didn't take a step back. Their bodies were inches away, one of his hands still resting above her hip.

"I'm glad you're okay," he said, his voice rough, his head bent toward her. Their gazes locked and held. Then his eyes skimmed lower, settling on her lips. Her breath hitched.

Moose got tired of lingering outside the barn and began plodding toward the entrance, breaking the spell. Lady started to follow, and Luke pulled Callie forward so she was out of the way. "They'll be looking for food and water," Luke said, releasing Callie. "Why don't I put them in the ties and then walk you up to the house? I can come back down and get them settled."

She shook her head. "I'm fine to stay. I'd like to help."

He looked at her for a moment, something like approval sliding over his handsome features. "If you're sure, that'd be great." With a conspiratorial smile, he added, "Then pie."

CHAPTER 9

*C*allie didn't end up getting home from the farm until shortly before she had to run back out to teach her class, so she decided to skip her cardio, despite feeling a little guilty about eating a slice of pie and then sharing Luke's second piece. Worth it, she decided as she let herself into her apartment. The pie really was indescribably delicious—Alice had salvaged all the cherries and still made two—but the banter with the two of them in the kitchen after the trail ride had fed a different need. One she hadn't realized she'd craved so desperately.

She'd go visit her father tomorrow, she decided as she locked the door behind her. He probably wouldn't recognize her, but it would be nice to see his kind face. To hold his hand.

Dropping her bag on a chair, she made her way into the little kitchen and opened the fridge. She hadn't had time to eat a proper dinner before class, and her stomach issued a plaintive growl as she perused her choices.

There was lettuce and half a yellow pepper on the bottom shelf; cherry tomatoes on the counter. That would do. She pulled everything out and set it on the counter, along with a cutting board and a bowl.

God, she was tired. Hopefully, the antagonistic ghost had spent all its energy today on messing up the flour message and scaring Lady and would leave Callie alone tonight. Exhaustion was seeping into her bones, and her muscles were beginning to ache in unusual places from the horseback ride.

She crunched a slice of pepper as she tore lettuce into pieces, debating what else she could add. Maybe some canned tuna? Pulling a can out of the pantry, she rummaged around for a can opener. As she closed the drawer, she popped a cherry tomato into her mouth.

Something smacked her between the shoulder blades, and she sucked in a stunned breath. The little tomato lodged in her throat as cold air surrounded her. She bent forward, trying to cough, but the tomato was stuck. She couldn't breathe. *Choking.*

She clutched at her neck, panic rising as her lungs began to burn. *Think!* Her phone was in her bag—she could call 911. She stumbled over toward the table on the other side of the kitchen counter.

How fast could they get here? She would lose consciousness any moment now. She would die. Her brain whirled as her lungs screamed. CPR. She was certified. Every year, in order to maintain her job as a fitness instructor. There was a way to administer the Heimlich to herself.

Instead of reaching into her bag, she lunged for the chair, yanking the back of it toward her. She clenched one shaking hand into a fist, wrapped the other hand around it, and positioned it between her ribcage and navel. Bracing her balled hands on the back of the chair, she thrust her upper body forward, driving her fist into her abdomen, over and over.

It wasn't working. She should have called an ambulance first. Now it was too late. Her vision turned cloudy, a rustle filled her ears. She was going to die.

She rammed her chest downward again with as much force as she could summon. The tomato flew out, along with a whoosh of air. Her body quaked as she sucked in oxygen, still bent over the chair. *It's out. I did it.*

Tears rolled down her face as she sank to the floor. She clutched the side rails of the chair and hung her head, sobbing quietly. Why was this happening to her? How could she make it stop?

It occurred to her that *thing* might still be here, watching her, gloating. Rage began to build, edging out fear. This ghost wasn't just trying to scare her. It was trying to *kill her*. This was war.

Sniffing back the last of the tears, she pulled herself up. If this spirit wanted to make her angry, it was working. She scanned the room as she wiped her eyes. Nothing that didn't belong, at least not that she could see. With cautious steps, she made her way back into the kitchen and filled a glass of water.

In some ways, the ghost had the upper hand. But it had limitations. It wasn't a physical being; it could only manage small manipulations in this world. Otherwise, it probably would have smothered her while she slept already. She shuddered, and the water sloshed as she sipped.

Every other ghost she'd encountered was lingering in between worlds in order to settle affairs from its life before. Why was this one here? And was Henry failing to move on because he needed to protect his family from a spirit with evil intentions?

A sharp ache throbbed between her temples, and she sighed. This wasn't going to stop until she figured out what was going on at Hillwood, and what needed to be done to put these spirits to rest. She would go over there tomorrow; she'd just sit out on the porch if she was in the way. But she needed to spend time there. Maybe there was some history on the farm that she could read.

What she needed now was sleep, which sounded absurd, considering the circumstances. But what else could she do? There was no running from this haunting—it had followed her here, it could follow her elsewhere. She wondered briefly if the ghost would eventually just leave her alone if she stayed away from Hillwood altogether. Frowning, she shook her head. She wasn't going to just abandon Alice. Or Luke. The thought of not seeing him again made a new ache open up in her chest.

She'd been given a gift—or a curse, depending on how you viewed it—and she was going to be the best candidate to solve this mystery. The haunting hadn't started with her, and she had no reason to think it would end if she extricated herself, even if the spirits stopped bothering her personally.

No hostile ghost was going to dictate her life. Setting down the water, she pulled out plastic wrap to cover the salad. Her appetite was gone, and the choking incident was too fresh. She wasn't going to soak in the tub tonight, either. Just brushing her teeth seemed like it would take all the energy she had.

She had to hope that this last burst of activity had drained the ghost's energy for the time being, too. From now on, she'd just have to be extra careful. And maybe she could take comfort in Henry's presence. He was trying to help them, she was sure of it. He just wasn't as strong as the other spirit. Not yet, anyway.

All was quiet as she got ready for bed. Too quiet. She flipped on the television, turning the volume down low. She was going to camp out on the couch again, she'd decided. For some reason, it felt safer, even if it probably didn't matter one bit where she slept. But it was near the front door, in the event she needed to run outside. She had her keys, her phone, and a flashlight on a small bench pushed up within arm's reach from the cushions. There was nothing more she could do tonight.

Settling her head on the pillow, she pulled up the blanket, aimed the remote at the TV, and searched for something pleasant that might lull her off to sleep.

CHAPTER 10

*H*e awoke from a dream about Callie, restless and hot. And aroused. Blood pulsed in his groin, and he sat up in bed with a groan. This was not good. He barely knew her. How had he gone from suspecting her of being a scam artist to having intense sex dreams about her in the span of two days? It was ridiculous.

And dangerous. He was not looking to get involved with anyone, after everything that had happened in his last relationship. That nightmare still made his stomach clench when he thought about it. Dragging a hand through his hair, he reached for the water bottle beside his bed.

He'd met Blair Adams at a bar, when he'd been out with Ryan one night last fall. It wasn't usually his way to pick up a girl at a bar and bring her home, but she'd been pretty and willing. More than willing, really—she'd invited herself over, leaving no doubt as to what she was looking for from him. And it hadn't been a one-night-stand; they'd enjoyed each other enough to start dating. She was fun, outgoing, and free-spirited. But she was also deeply disturbed, he discovered later.

There was a side of her that was needy and paranoid. Wildly jealous. She would go through his things, look at his phone, and follow him to construction sites, convinced he was cheating. He wasn't cheating, but he was growing tired of her accusations. Attempts to spend time apart were met with hysteria. When he broke up with her, she refused to accept it. She showed up at his house in the middle of the night. She stalked him at work. She even spun a false story about her mother dying to gain his sympathy; he found out later her mother was alive and well, living in Florida. In fact, he'd spoken to Blair's mother as he unraveled the lies, and she had warned him of her daughter's emotional troubles. Apparently, Blair had been in and out of hospitals as a teen.

He shook his head at the memory, gulping more water. He'd finally threatened to file a restraining order before she'd given up. What a fiasco.

So, no one could blame him for being gun-shy. His last relationship had been a chaotic roller coaster with an exhausting break-up that stretched through most of the month of February. And then his Pop had died just a few weeks later, sending his own family into a tailspin. He hadn't had time to think about dating, even if he'd been interested.

Then Callie had shown up, and suddenly he couldn't get her out of his mind. Clearly, his subconscious has some lustful ideas about her. But he didn't know her, not really.

She claimed to be a psychic, for God's sake. After everything he'd been through, there was no way he was going to get involved with a woman convinced she talked to ghosts.

Taking her to bed doesn't necessarily require a relationship, a selfish inner voice pointed out in an echo of Ryan's comment from the other night. He shut it down with a disgusted sigh. First of all, there was no indication she wanted to jump into bed with him. Secondly, something told him he couldn't have sex with Callie and not form an emotional bond. Hell, he already seemed to be forming one. He'd had fun with her today. His heart had seized when her horse had reared. And now he was sitting up in bed in the middle of the night, thinking about her. Or rather, trying not to think about her.

Throwing off the covers, he made his way through the familiar darkness to the hallway. He flicked on the bathroom lights and froze.

Every drawer in the sink vanity had been pulled out; all four cabinet doors beneath stood open.

He blinked, dragging a hand over his eyes. But it didn't help—the bathroom was still in a strange state of disarray. What the hell?

Leaning against the doorway, he tried to make sense of it. He was certain none of the drawers and doors had been left open when he'd finished in the bathroom before heading to bed. Definitely not all of them. He was the only one who used this bathroom—the master bedroom that had been added over the garage had its own bath. His Gram used that. Even if she had needed something in this bathroom, there was no way she would have rummaged through the drawers and left every single one open. Gram was neat and orderly.

Unless...maybe she'd been sleepwalking?

He frowned, entering the room and staring at the open drawers. Nothing had been tossed about inside. So strange. Pressing his lips together, he closed everything quietly, then rested his palms on the cool counter of the vanity. He bent his head, blew out a breath.

The conversation he'd had with Gram and Callie in the kitchen, before the trail ride, drifted through his mind. The conviction in their voices had told him they absolutely believed there were spirits lurking around the farm. Callie's eyes had glittered with real fear when she'd described her ordeal at her apartment. He no longer believed Gram was imagining that things had been moved because she missed Pop so much. Wishful thinking of some sort; an attempt to maintain a connection with her beloved husband. And he didn't think Callie was simply looking to exploit Alice anymore.

But could he bring himself to believe in ghosts? Was this an attempt by Pop, or the other supposed phantom, to convince him they existed?

Gram sleepwalking made more sense.

He finished in the bathroom, glancing back to make sure everything was still as he'd left it before he shut off the light. A single thought kept niggling at him, demanding attention.

He'd never known Gram to sleepwalk. Not only had he never witnessed it in all the years he'd spent nights at Hillwood; she'd never once mentioned it was something she did. Nor had anyone in the family ever referenced it.

Well, there was a first time for everything. Hell, maybe he'd just taken his initial foray into sleepwalking and done it himself, earlier in the night. As disturbing as that idea was, he preferred it to the ghost theory.

He crushed his head into the pillow and grimaced as he twisted beneath the sheets. Squeezing his eyes shut, he willed sleep to come and take him. A heavy, dreamless slumber, the kind that didn't allow for unconscious excursions throughout the house or steamy thoughts of Callie.

CHAPTER 11

*S*he'd made it through the night. Again. But her eyes felt gritty, her head foggy.

She didn't believe for one moment the cruel spirit seemingly intent on hurting her had decided to just leave her alone. More likely, it had expended all its energy and needed to recharge. Or, Henry's ghost was challenging it, thwarting some of its violent actions. Maybe both. She sent up a silent prayer of thanks to Henry, just in case, as she cracked eggs into a bowl.

Once she'd cooked her breakfast and sat down to eat, she chewed each bite cautiously, her phone on the table, 9-1 punched into the keypad. "What a way to live," she said to the empty apartment when she'd finished with no supernatural interruptions. With a sigh, she took her dishes to the sink, cleaning up in the kitchen before jumping in the shower.

An hour later, she pulled out of the parking lot of her complex, her car packed with everything she could think of that she might need for the day: purse, laptop, the Dragonfly Kingdom books, a few snacks, and a thermos of coffee. She was hoping to avoid her apartment for the longest stretch of time possible before she had to return tonight.

As she waited at the light to turn onto Route 28, she dug out her phone and pressed Alice's number. Voicemail picked up, and Callie couldn't help smiling at Alice's tentative instructions to leave a message at the beep. She asked if she could come over later to spend time at the house, then ended the call.

A light rain misted the windshield as she arrived at the assisted living facility where her father had lived for the last four years. The memory care center had its own private entrance, with security measures to keep residents suffering from dementia from wandering off unaccompanied. Callie pulled into a parking space and hurried to the entrance, her shoulders hunched, the Dragonfly books clutched to her chest to keep them dry.

Once she was in the building, she trudged the familiar path to her father's room, which was a "companion suite"— one small common area, one bathroom, and two small bedrooms with separate entrances along the hallway. She wished he had a private room, but it was the best she could do, given the astronomical costs of this type of care. All the proceeds from the sale of their old house had gone into an account to help pay the bills; the money was dwindling quicker than Callie had expected.

Callie's mom, Joy, had helped her set everything up, when it became clear she wasn't going to win her battle with cancer. When Thomas was first diagnosed with Early Onset Alzheimer's Disease, at the age of 57, they did everything they could to attempt to slow the symptoms and keep him at home. But by the time Callie was in college, Thomas was becoming a danger to himself, wandering away from home and getting lost, turning appliances on and forgetting about them, even threatening Andrew with a knife when he failed to recognize Callie's boyfriend of five years. Both Callie and Joy knew it was time to explore a safer environment for him, as heartbreaking as it was. Then, with Joy's own bleak prognosis looming, the situation became urgent.

"Good morning, Thomas," Callie said brightly as she stood in the doorway to the tiny private area of his bedroom. She'd learned using his name was a better way to greet him, as opposed to calling him 'Dad'. Less confusion. Less distress.

He was propped up in bed, staring at the television. Blinking, he turned his head toward her, his wrinkled brow furrowing deeper. His expression remained clouded as she entered the room, but then his eyes widened a bit, the watery green flickering with a hint of recognition. "Joy?"

He thought she was her mother. It happened often, and it was fine. Much better than not being recognized as anyone.

"Hi," she responded softly as she entered, neither agreeing or disagreeing with his uncertain identification. "Is it okay if I turn this off?" She tipped her chin toward the TV. "I thought we could read together." Approaching the bed, she held up the first volume of the book series they'd so painstakingly put together all those years ago. The paper was worn and dog-eared, the once-vibrant hues of the illustrations faded with age.

Thomas cocked his head, a thoughtful look on his face as he examined the dark-haired fairy princess riding a colorful dragonfly on the book's cover. Eventually he nodded, his mouth quivering slightly, and he settled his clasped hands on his chest.

She aimed the remote at the TV, and the daytime talk show disappeared from the screen. Her throat tightened with emotion as she pulled a chair next to the bed, and she swallowed hard to clear it. Bringing her head close to his, she began reading the words she knew by heart.

SHE'D HOPED to take her father for a walk around the gardens if the sky cleared up, but he'd fallen asleep as she read. Taking his hand in hers, she'd leaned back in her chair and closed her eyes for a quick rest. A return call from Alice had jarred her awake over an hour later, but the ringtone hadn't disturbed Thomas's slumber. The disease took its toll on the body as well as the mind.

So she'd kissed his papery cheek goodbye and left the room, stopping in the lobby to use the bathroom and listen to Alice's message. Callie was welcome at Hillwood anytime, Alice insisted in her voicemail.

She'd stopped for a late lunch at a popular café, making sure to sit in clear view of other customers and employees, in case the ghost decided to pull any tricks. When she'd finished, she drove to the farm, rolling her neck and shoulders at every stoplight to try to work the kinks out. A series of cracking sounds accompanied every move, and she winced. After two nights on the couch, a nap in a chair, and a trail ride culminating in nearly being thrown from a horse, what she needed was a massage. Shaking her head, she huffed out something between a sigh and a chuckle. How about a spa week at an exclusive five-star resort while she was at it? Both things were in about similar reach, financially.

Now, she was sitting on the porch of Hillwood, admiring the uninterrupted expanse of open fields and the still, sunlit water of the lake. This morning's misty rain had swept farther inland, dragging the humidity with it. A crisp breeze carried the briny scent of the ocean with it as it stirred her hair. Pulling it into her lungs, she closed her eyes and allowed herself a moment to savor it. It would be beach weather soon. *Here's hoping I live long enough to see it.*

When she opened her eyes, her gaze fell back on the papers stacked on her lap. Alice had dug through Henry's desk and pulled out a few folders filled with documents on Hillwood Farm. The rest of the stack waited on a table beside her chair, along with a glass of lemonade that tasted a lot like fresh-squeezed.

Footsteps thudded up onto the side porch from over near the garage, and she was amazed at the warm familiarity the sound invoked. *Luke.* She allowed a goofy grin to play across her lips for the brief moment before he appeared around the corner. She couldn't control the butterflies, though. They danced through her belly with giddy abandon. Oh, Lord. She was in trouble.

He stopped short when he saw her. "Oh, hey. I didn't know you were here."

"I asked Alice if I could come over and look at old files. I thought it might help."

Nodding, he raised his hand to rub the back of his neck, revealing dried streaks of something white along the inside of his arm. Splotches of whatever it was dotted the lower half of his faded navy T-shirt, which had "Turner Construction" emblazoned across the chest and frayed edges where the sleeves had been cut off.

She was staring, she realized. And he was staring back, as if waiting for her to elaborate. She lifted the papers on her lap to illustrate her project. "It's paperwork on the farm. I thought it might be helpful, like maybe I might find some kind of clue." Now she was repeating herself. And, she sounded like Nancy Drew. But she couldn't seem to stop. "I'm quickly realizing it's a road to nowhere, though. Even if I find a record of someone connected to Hillwood who died in a significant way, why would that person's ghost have hung around all this time, only to make trouble now? It makes no sense. Unless maybe your grandfather's ghost has stirred something up."

His brows furrowed as he pressed his lips together.

"I think I'll just have to wait for more messages, if they can get through," she finished, nearly breathless. What was wrong with her? Stop talking. She reached for the glass of lemonade, sliding her gaze to his face as she sipped.

She expected to see derision painted across his handsome features, as plain as the white plaster streaking his arms. But his expression was neutral. "Well, let me know if you find anything interesting," he said, without a hint of contempt in his voice. If anything, he sounded sincere.

"I will," she confirmed. "And apparently there are some boxes in the attic I could look through too, just in case. Although Alice forbade me from going up and carrying them down myself."

The corner of his mouth quirked up. "Am I the volunteer for that job?"

She laughed. "Yes."

He rolled his eyes skyward, crossing his arms and rocking back on his heels. But his expression made it clear he was only feigning annoyance. "No problem. Will you be around for a while?"

"Actually, Alice invited me to stay for dinner." Callie had been hesitant to accept at first, but the kitchen had smelled so good. Not to mention, eating with other people seemed prudent after last night. And she didn't have to teach a class tonight, either. "So, yes," she finished.

He cocked his head, brows lifting as he peered down at her. "Oh, I see now. You're in this for the pie."

As she broke into laughter again, she suddenly realized how long it had been since she'd laughed this much. And how good it felt. She'd known Luke for just three days, but being around him made her feel...lighter. Despite everything going on, despite the fact that she was hanging around his family's farmhouse hoping to connect with a ghost, or maybe even two ghosts, Luke was somehow able to make her laugh. He was amazing.

And single, her inner voice reminded her.

She tamped down the thought immediately. Guys like Luke weren't interested in introverts with tragic pasts who talked to restless spirits. Not romantically, anyway. He was simply a nice guy, and she should be grateful for that. She was lucky he was willing to stand here and joke around with her, given the circumstances.

"I do like the pie," she admitted, unable to suppress a smile. But uncertainty set in on the tails of her sharp inner dialog, and she added, "Anyway, I accepted the invitation. I hope you don't mind."

He gave her a playful smirk, dimples flashing. "Of course not." He ran his hand through his already tousled hair. "No doubt Gram is thrilled to be having company aside from me," he added with a chuckle.

"She did seem a bit excited."

"Well, I'll go grab those boxes while I'm a mess. Then I'll get cleaned up."

Images of him in the shower suddenly flashed through her mind, and she cut her gaze away from his silvery blue eyes before he could read her thoughts. Good Lord. Swallowing, she pretended to focus on arranging the papers she'd been reading. "Okay, great. Do you need any help?"

"Nah, I'll manage."

She nodded as she peeked back up at him. "Thanks. Sorry to add to your workload."

He lifted a muscled shoulder. "No worries. I'll leave them in the front hall."

Her body went limp as he disappeared into the house,

and she exhaled, melting into the chair. A trickle of perspiration slid down the column of her spine. Great.

Maybe you should go join him in the shower, the cheeky inner voice suggested.

Maybe you should shut up. And now she was talking to herself, which wasn't completely out of the ordinary, but it was still alarming, considering she wasn't at home. At least she wasn't actually saying the comments out loud.

But the bigger point was that she was supposed to be working. Of course she was latching onto distractions—so far, the information in this paperwork was dry as dust and not at all helpful. That didn't mean there wasn't something useful in here, though, waiting to be discovered. A spirit was threatening her life; another was possibly trying to shed light on who it was and how to stop it. Her attention needed to be on this, and nothing else, unless she wanted to continue being held hostage to fear and violence.

Bending her head, she gripped the papers with her sweaty hands as she resumed poring over the documents. After a few pages, her vision began to swim, until her eyes caught on something that sent a prickle of excitement through her veins.

CHAPTER 12

*D*inner tasted as good as it had smelled—homemade meatloaf, fresh bread right out of the bread maker, and crisp green beans. Plus, there *was* pie to look forward to for dessert.

Callie savored a bite of warm bread slathered with butter, nearly moaning with pleasure. So good. Alice had insisted on opening a bottle of Zinfandel, even though Luke was drinking beer, and as Callie took another sip of the tart ruby wine, she could feel her muscles relaxing. It was almost unsettling how much this dinner meant to her. Not just the food and the wine, but the company. The effortless way Alice and Luke included her, as if she belonged here.

After the initial conversation about the food dwindled, Alice raised her own glass and gestured toward Callie. "So, dear, did you find anything out today?"

Two pairs of matching gray-blue eyes settled on her, and she flushed. Suddenly self-conscious, she lifted the napkin from her lap and wiped her lips. "Maybe. It's pretty thin, though." She shrugged, picking up the bread and tearing off a piece to keep her hands busy. "Apparently there was an employee who worked on the farm in the 1950s who lost his arm in a hay baler accident. He survived, but at this point, he's almost certainly passed on, so there's that. I did a search on his name, but it's so common, I didn't get very far. The thing is...his first name was Robert. Robert Smith. And 'R' could have been the letter Henry was trying to write."

Luke set his beer down, nodding thoughtfully. "I remember that story, although I didn't know the guy's name. Pop drilled the gruesome details into our heads as kids to reinforce the idea that the tools and machines around here are dangerous."

"I remember it too," added Alice. "Awful. But...why now? Are you thinking maybe he passed away recently, and decided to come take out his anger over losing his arm?"

"It's possible," said Callie as she chewed the bread. A small part of her was waiting for the forceful blow to her back, but the alcohol certainly helped keep her anxiety at bay. "It's just that I can't imagine him being angry enough to try to kill me."

Silence.

Whoops. She realized her mistake immediately; she hadn't told them yet about last night's choking incident. It wasn't that she planned to keep it a secret...she just wasn't sure how to broach the subject correctly. She didn't want to downplay it, exactly, but she also didn't want to be overly dramatic. Especially when she was getting along so well with Luke, because this story would certainly make him suspicious of her all over again. There was no way he was going to believe a ghost hit her in the back with the intention of making her choke while she was alone. He'd think she was seeking attention, or money, or maybe he'd just decide she was flat-out crazy.

Well, it was done now. The wine had loosened her tongue; she couldn't take it back. And you couldn't get much more dramatic than announcing a ghost was trying to kill you.

She squirmed beneath their stunned scrutiny, ripping the soft bread into little white fragments. *Stop.*

Luke finally spoke. "Callie, what do you mean? Did something else happen to you that we don't know about?"

"Um…well, last night, while I was making dinner, I was snacking on cherry tomatoes. And…something…hit me in the back, right as I put a tomato in my mouth, and I choked. But I'm fine now," she added hurriedly, reaching for her wine glass.

Alice's face was white as a sheet. "What exactly do you mean by choked? Could you breathe?"

Swallowing a sip, she cleared her throat. "No. But I was able to give myself CPR—the Heimlich, actually—and it came out and I was fine."

Both their jaws dropped. "You…gave yourself the Heimlich?" asked Luke slowly. Rigid tendons formed cords along his neck.

"Did you call an ambulance?" Alice's voice trembled as she asked her question almost simultaneously.

Crap. This was not a subject she wanted to dwell on.

They'd been having such a nice time, and she may have found a promising lead. "Yes, I'm trained in CPR and I remembered how to do the Heimlich on myself," she said with a little nod of confirmation. "So, no, I didn't need to call an ambulance. Like I said, I was okay, and it was late. There was nothing paramedics could have done at that point, really."

Luke pinned her with a steady gaze. "You're saying it wasn't an accident, though, right?"

She shrugged. "I mean...I guess it could have been." *No.* She was diminishing what had happened. "Actually, no," she said aloud, shifting in her chair. "It wasn't an accident. I definitely felt a blow to my back, and I think it was timed to have the effect that it did. But please, I don't want to ruin this delicious dinner talking about it anymore. Truly. Let's enjoy the food." With forced casualness, she speared a green bean.

Alice made a small, noncommittal sound as she reached for her wine. She straightened her shoulders, looking directly across the table at Callie. "Maybe you should come stay with us," she said, lifting the glass to her lips.

Now it was Callie's turn to go still. Her mouth fell open as she tried to process the words. She flicked a glance to the head of the table—Luke appeared equally surprised. What to say? "Oh, no," she managed, shaking her head. "Thank you very much for the offer, but I couldn't do that."

"Why not? There are two more empty bedrooms upstairs. I'd feel better if you were around people while this is going on. You'd be safer." That familiar determination was creeping back into Alice's tone.

Callie's chest tightened as gratitude welled up inside her. But she was not going to foist herself on this family any more than she already had. God, she couldn't even imagine what Luke was thinking right now. "Really, thank you, but I'm okay at my apartment." She popped a bite of meatloaf into her mouth as if this were a perfectly normal dinner conversation.

Lines furrowed across Alice's forehead. "Well, the offer stands. I know you said you lost your mom a few years ago, and that your dad's in a nursing home, so if you change your mind, you're welcome here."

Luke turned toward Callie. "I'm sorry about your family. I didn't know that," he said, his voice low and edged with sympathy.

"Thanks," she nearly whispered past the lump in her throat. The sting of tears gathered behind her eyes, and she cast about frantically for anything to change the subject. She was not going to cry in the middle of this nice dinner. She already felt like she'd ruined the meal.

A sudden grinding rumble made them all jump in their seats, and Callie's pulse leapt as she looked around in confusion.

"It's just the overhead garage door," explained Luke, rising from his chair. "It's been acting up lately. I just can't figure out what's wrong with it." He strode from the dining hall through the kitchen and down the back hallway. A few moments later, the rumble repeated as the door shut down. Luke paused at the fridge on his way back to pull out another beer. "Has to be something going on with the sensor," he said as twisted off the cap and sat back down.

Judging from Alice's expression, she wasn't buying that explanation for a second. But she didn't comment, only stood and refilled Callie's wine glass, then her own. With a stoic smile, she gestured toward everyone's plates. "Does anyone need anything else? Don't forget we have pie, too."

They managed to swing the conversation to current events and an offer Luke received on the house he put up for sale, and the tension eased as they finished their meal. But after dessert, Alice quietly reiterated her offer while Callie stood beside her at the sink. "You're welcome to stay here anytime, if you change your mind."

Callie dried a serving bowl with a dish towel. "Thank you."

"We should make sure you have Luke's number, too. He's better at keeping his phone with him. That way, if something happens, you can call him."

She set the bowl on the counter. "Oh, I don't know...," she began, trailing off.

"It's fine," Alice insisted, her voice firm. "Even if it's the middle of the night, I want you to promise to call if you need him."

Part of her brain went rogue, conjuring up a forbidden image of Luke showing up in the middle of the night at her bidding. Heat licked at her cheeks. Maybe that second glass of wine hadn't been the best idea. She realized Alice was waiting for a response, so she did her best to clear her mind of the steamy scenario currently playing out and murmured, "I promise." Opening the cabinet above, she pulled out a glass and crossed the kitchen to fill it at the fridge's water dispenser.

As she stood there, Luke came up beside her, and she caught a hint of his now-familiar scent—a devastatingly masculine combination of soap, leather, and wood. She inhaled, savoring it for a moment before she could stop herself. Then he touched the small of her back, and her heart skittered.

"Join me for a walk?" His hand lingered for a beat before falling away.

Oh, God. For a moment, she literally couldn't speak. Why would he want to invite her on a walk? Because he was interested in her? No, that couldn't be it. To tell her once and for all to take her ridiculous claims and peddle them somewhere else? More likely.

But then again, he'd touched her. It was probably nothing—a gesture to get her attention. But for some reason, it felt intimate. And, oh, so good.

She pushed away the chaotic thoughts and focused on forming a coherent response. "That'd be great," she managed. There. Nothing wrong with that. An after-dinner walk around a beautiful farm *was* great.

And the company wasn't bad, either.

He nodded, turning toward Alice. "Gram, we're going to go for a walk before I take care of the horses for the night."

Warm blood rushed to Callie's face, and she gulped at her water. "Is there anything else that needs to be done first?"

Alice shooed them away with a wave of her hand. "I can finish up anything that needs doing. You young people go. It's Friday night, for goodness sake."

"Ready?" Luke asked.

"Ready." She pulled in a breath, hoping her hand appeared steady as she set down her glass. Combing her hair back with her fingers, she followed Luke toward the front door.

The sun had already slipped behind the tree line, leaving amber streaks across the indigo sky. A silvery half-moon glowed in the falling darkness, joined by a few bright stars. The cool night air carried the scents of their surroundings—the fields, the woods, the barn. Tiny creatures swooped overhead, and she had a feeling they were bats. Which was fine. She wasn't afraid of bats. There were much scarier things in her world.

"Let's go down to the pond," Luke said, leading them along the walkway toward the side of the house.

As they passed the garage, she tensed, praying one of the overhead doors wouldn't suddenly come to life and darken the mood. But they both stayed closed against the night, sheltering Alice's car, while her car and Luke's truck sat side-by-side in the wide parking area. Moths fluttered around the two outdoor lights in frantic circles.

The shortest distance to the water was straight down the grassy hill to their left, but it was a steeper slope than the curved drive down to the barn, so they continued along the driveway as the asphalt turned to packed dirt. Light stretched out from the open entrance to the barn, and a trio of horses stood near the building in the back field.

"Are they waiting for you?" she asked.

He rubbed the back of his neck. "Probably. I fed them at 4:00, but they get hay and water to last them through the night when I put them into their stalls. They're creatures of habit. They know where to find the outdoor hay feeder if they're really hungry. They just know the routine. I usually do the night check around 8:00 or 9:00."

"That must put a damper on your weekend nights." What a dumb thing to say. It was none of her business, and it had to be crystal clear she was fishing to see if he had a date tonight. "I mean, unless you go out after," she added quickly.

He chuckled. "Fortunately, that's not a big concern of mine right now. Too much going on these days, and I get up so early that late nights at bars are not as appealing as they used to be." There was a pause as they reached the bottom of the hill. "Are you headed out tonight?"

She nearly burst out laughing, which would have been better, because instead what came out was a cross between a giggle and a snort. Lovely. "No. Definitely not. I rarely go out on the weekends." Very true, if rarely meant 'never'. When her father had begun to show symptoms, she'd decided to continue living at home and attend college nearby. Of course, Andrew's decision to also enroll at Bridgewater State University played a part. During those four years, she and Andrew became their own social circle, and her high school friendships fell by the wayside. Then her mother passed away from cancer her senior year in college; one year later, the accident took Andrew's life and changed her own life forever.

So, no...even if she wanted to go out, she wouldn't have anyone to go out with at this point. Every once in a while, some of the other instructors at the gym proposed a

Ladies' Night, but Callie had declined enough times now that she was probably no longer invited to the gatherings, if they still took place. It wasn't that she disliked the women—she just didn't want to get close enough to attract their dead relatives. Not to mention public places could also be fraught with desperate spirits seeking a messenger. All things she preferred to avoid, if possible.

Unless it was under her terms. Like Hillwood.

"What's a usual weekend night for you, then?" he asked, leading them toward the same path they'd ridden on yesterday, alongside the split rail fence.

"Popcorn and TV," she replied. "Boring, I know. Although sometimes I'll order a movie, if I'm feeling really wild."

He joined her laughter. "Not boring at all. It sounds perfect, actually."

Her stomach flipped. Was he being serious? And if so, was he picturing the two of them curled up on a couch together, like she currently was? No, of course not. Ridiculous.

His fingers grazed her arm as he steered them off the path toward the pond. The symphony of bullfrogs and crickets grew louder as they approached the bank. Moonlight shimmered over the still water.

They strolled along the bank in companionable silence for a few minutes, taking in the tranquil setting. The long grass whispered as it brushed against their calves, and grasshoppers whirred out of the way of their footsteps.

"Does it have a name? The pond?" she eventually asked, her voice only slightly above a whisper. Somehow that seemed appropriate, as if talking loudly might be disruptive in a place that deserved reverence.

He gave a low chuckle. "A very original one. Turner Pond."

She laughed softly along with him. "I guess that makes sense, since your family has owned this property for so long." Pausing, she added, "I really hope you're able to save it. It's beautiful here."

"Thanks. I'm going to do everything in my power to keep it off the auction block." He cleared his throat. "I'm really sorry about your family. I didn't know about your parents."

"Thanks," she echoed. She looked up at him as they walked, studying his profile in the shadows. "My mother passed away three years ago from cancer. And my father was diagnosed with early-onset Alzheimer's when he was in his late 50s. He's in a memory care center now. I was there earlier today, visiting. He doesn't recognize me anymore." An ache spread through her chest like a gaping hole. She swallowed back a sob, brushing at an insect hovering by her ear.

"Wow, that's rough. Do you have any siblings?"

"No. My parents had me later in life. They didn't think they could have children at all, but then I came along."

"They must have been so happy."

Her lips curved into a sad smile. "They were. The three of us were really close. The time we did have together was full of love and happiness, so I try to hang onto that."

"You should. Family's important." As they rounded the

far edge of the pond, he motioned toward a small pier extending out into the water.

"It is," she agreed. She wasn't really sure why she felt comfortable sharing these details with him. Maybe it was the darkness, draped around them like a protective blanket. Or the isolation, the sense of being the only two people in the world. Maybe it was everything they'd been through together in the last few days, somehow making her feel as if she'd known him for a much longer time.

"I've always felt closest to my Gram and Pop," he admitted, leading her onto the wooden pier. The boards creaked softly beneath their footsteps.

Maybe he felt it too…some sort of fragile bond developing between them.

"Don't get me wrong, I love my parents," he continued as they gazed out over the water. "And I know they love me, and would do anything for me. But I think I'm more like my grandparents. My mother is more about appearances. About fitting into the right circles at the country club."

A loud splash rang out beside the pier, and she jumped. He reached out to steady her, pulling her away from the edge, toward him. She bumped against the solid mass of his chest, her breath catching.

"Whoa," he said, his fingers wrapped around her upper arm in a firm grip. "Can't have you going over. It's still pretty cold."

"Sorry," she said, looking up at him. "I'm a bit…jumpy these days."

"That's understandable." He held her gaze, not releasing her.

Her pulse raced in her veins, hot and thick, and she knew it wasn't just the result of a momentary startle. His free hand moved up toward her face, and time slowed as he tucked her hair behind her ear. Her lungs stopped working. Then his palm slid back behind her head, anchoring her, as he bent toward her.

His lips brushed against hers, sending a series of fiery tremors through her. Oh my God. She leaned into him, slipping her hands around his waist. As he deepened the kiss, he pulled her closer, curling a strong arm around her back.

Desire surged through her body like an electrical current. His teeth grazed her lower lip, and her knees turned liquid.

Another splash, forceful enough to send droplets of water onto the pier, broke into the moment, bringing them both back to reality. Her muscles tensed, and she eased away slightly, turning her face away from his to look out over the pond. "Are there fish in there?" she asked, struggling to get her mind working again. Had that really just happened?

His hands settled on her shoulders before sliding down and falling away. "Yes," he confirmed, his voice husky and faraway. "Fish, frogs, turtles."

She nodded, her fingers drifting to her tingling lips. She felt woozy. "Whatever it was sounded big."

He made a low sound of agreement, following her gaze

along the surface of the water. "I've seen muskrats in there too."

She wasn't quite sure how they went from kissing to muskrats, but she was pretty sure it was her fault. There was no denying the small wave of relief, though, mixed in with all the other emotions coursing through her. Her thoughts were spinning. Her body was pulsing. She was confused, tired, and worried that whatever had made those noises wasn't part of the natural aquatic wildlife population. Maybe she was being paranoid, but she had good reason.

"I should probably get going. Let you take care of the horses."

"Right. Listen, Callie...I don't want you to think I asked you to come down here so I could..." He trailed off, raking a hand through his hair. "I asked you to come on a walk because I wanted to apologize."

"Apologize?" She rubbed her forehead, as if she could physically clear the fog from her brain.

He tipped his head toward the bank of the pond, and they started walking slowly back to where the pier joined the field. "Yes. For the comments I made when we first met." He blew out a breath. "I'm still having trouble with the ghost thing, even though I'm trying to keep an open mind. But I don't believe you're trying to con my grandmother out of money, and I'm sorry I accused you of that."

Whoa. This night just kept getting more surreal. Her chest tightened, and she blinked rapidly as tears threatened to fall. "Thanks. I would never do that."

"I know that now."

"I'm glad. I know it's hard to believe all this. I didn't believe it, either, until enough things happened to make it impossible for me to deny. But as long as you believe I'm only trying to help, that's all that matters."

"I do. And I'm going to try to be supportive. And keep an open mind, like I said."

A flood of gratitude swept over her, and she barely managed to get the word 'thanks' past the lump in her throat. He was accepting her, and trusting her, if not outright believing in her ability to communicate with ghosts. It was enough. It was…a lot.

A fourth horse had joined the group outside the barn; their silhouettes formed majestic curves and lines beneath the moonlight. "Where are the other two?" she asked, hoping to move the conversation back to a safe, practical subject.

"They could be in their stalls already, if the back doors to the field were open. Or they could be beneath the shed, where the feeder is. If not, a few whistles will bring them. Horses are pack animals. They generally want to be with the herd."

"What about the other animals? The cats?"

"Oh, I feed them too. But they do their own thing. Most of them have just shown up, decided the barn was a good place to live, and settled in."

She smiled in the darkness. "That's nice of you to feed them."

He lifted a shoulder. "They'd probably do okay on their own. But yeah, it's not a lot of extra work to leave a bowl of cat food out."

They were back at the corner of the fence, where the dirt driveway split around to the barn, or over to the house. She hesitated, then asked, "Do you need any help?"

With a small smile, he shook his head. "No, I got it. But thanks. I think I need to get you back up to Gram before she starts worrying. I'll walk you up."

Her heartrate picked back up. "Oh, you don't need to do that. I'm fine. You have things to do."

"I'll walk you," he repeated, his tone holding no room for argument.

"Okay. Thanks." She supposed they were facing an awkward goodbye scene wherever they parted. Her fingers twisted together as they climbed the hill.

But Alice saved her. When they approached the house, Alice was outside the garage, depositing the empty beer bottles into the plastic recycling bin. "Oh, you're back! How was your walk?" she asked, her wide smile evident in the glow of the outdoor lights.

Did she know? Callie ducked her head, hoping the flush of her cheeks wasn't visible in the shadows. This was getting more and more complicated. She prayed the older woman wasn't hoping for a romance to bloom between Callie and her grandson. As attracted as she was to Luke, there was no possibility of an actual relationship there. She'd already found—and lost—her soulmate. She'd lost everyone she loved. In her experience, love equaled pain, and her heart had been through too much to risk any more.

And despite the kiss, Luke probably had no interest in actually getting involved with her. No one in their right mind would, once they got a preview of all the baggage she came with.

She suddenly realized Alice was waiting for an answer, and she pulled herself back from her spiraling thoughts. "It was great."

"Gram, I would have done that," Luke said.

Alice rolled her eyes. "I think I can handle it," she countered with mock exasperation. But a hint of appreciation mingled with the playfulness in her voice. She dusted her palms, as if signaling she'd finished with a tough job.

"Just leave anything else for me, Gram. I'll get to it after I'm done in the barn."

"It's all done," Alice replied. She turned her gaze to Callie. "Are you sure you don't want to stay?"

You should stay. Say yes. Out loud, she said, "Thanks, but I'm fine. I should get going, actually. I just need to get my stuff together."

"I'll be back up in a few, Gram," Luke said as he took a step backward. "'Night, Callie." He turned and strode down the hill.

Stealing one last glimpse of his retreating form, she followed Alice into the house.

CHAPTER 13

*B*y Sunday night, Luke was forced to admit he missed Callie. Which was ridiculous; he'd seen her on Friday night. Seen her—and kissed her, he reminded himself as he checked his phone. What had he been thinking? After everything that had happened with Blair, he should have learned his lesson about allowing impulse to take over. But that's exactly what he'd done. It was true that he'd only asked her to go on a walk so he could apologize. Something had come over him in that moment on the pier, and he simply hadn't had the willpower to fight the attraction. He'd suddenly *had* to feel her lips beneath his, to feel her body close to his. It had been a desire too strong to resist.

And she'd kissed him back.

He glanced between the Red Sox game on TV and his phone, thumbing through screens. Double-checking, for the hundredth time this weekend, to make sure Callie hadn't texted him. Gram had put his number into her phone before she'd left, apparently, and told her to get in touch with him if she needed something and couldn't reach Alice.

So, Callie had his number. But he didn't have hers.

The very fact that he was worried about her bothered him on multiple levels. For starters, he barely knew her. Plus, he didn't want to get emotionally involved with anyone right now.

But the more troubling piece was *why* he was worried. Did it mean he believed she was in danger? By extension, did it mean he believed in ghosts?

He'd promised he'd keep an open mind. His mind, however, kept reminding him that most of the strange things Callie and Gram were attributing to ghosts could have logical explanations. Items fell off walls sometimes. Papers got misplaced. Drawers got left open by mistake. People sleepwalked. Things broke. Flour could spill in a pattern that resembled a letter. Accidents happened.

People choked.

That's it. He sprang up from the couch and strode out of the living room. He found Gram in the dining room, the Sunday paper spread out on the table, a glass of water and a bowl of nuts in reach. She looked up at him as he entered. "How's the game?"

It took him a moment. "Oh. Good. Red Sox are up." He squeezed her shoulder gently as he passed on his way to the refrigerator. Pulling out a beer, he twisted off the cap and took a long pull. "Have you heard from Callie at all?" he asked as nonchalantly as he could manage.

She studied him for a moment from behind her reading

glasses. Lifting up the scattered papers, she located her phone and glanced at the screen. "I spoke with her last this afternoon. So far, she said everything's been relatively quiet at her apartment this weekend."

He pressed his lips together. What did 'relatively quiet' mean? "Well, that's good."

"Yes. It's been quiet here, too. Even ghosts get tired, apparently."

Or maybe they're conserving energy for something bigger. The thought sent anxiety thrumming through his veins. He leaned against the edge of the counter with forced casualness, hoping Gram would volunteer to give Callie a quick call. Their gazes held for a few beats.

"I can give you her number if you'd like to check in with her yourself," Gram finally suggested. "I'm sure she'd appreciate that."

He wasn't entirely sure she would, but…screw it. With a sigh, he opened his contacts and handed his phone to her.

A sly smile tugged at the corners of her mouth as she punched the information in with one finger. Adjusting her glasses to double-check the digits, she nodded and passed it back to him. "Let me know what she says."

He scowled as he walked out of the dining room. Great. If Gram thought she was being subtle, she was mistaken. As he returned to the living room, he glanced over at the TV to check the score. And came to a sudden stop.

The television hung on the wall above the fireplace now; he'd bought the large flat screen for Gram and Pop one Christmas and hung it himself. A wooden cabinet sat to the right of the fireplace, the cable box resting on top.

Inside the cabinet, old DVDs occupied one shelf, intricate jigsaw puzzles were stacked on the bottom.

The two cabinet doors stood wide open. Both of them. And he was absolutely certain they'd been closed when he'd left the room. He would have noticed otherwise, lounging on the couch across from it, pointing the remote directly at it.

The hairs on his arms prickled, and then he noticed how cold it was—as if the temperature in the room had dropped significantly in the few minutes he'd been away. He slowly turned his head back toward the front door, to make sure it wasn't open.

Closed. His gaze swept the windows overlooking the front porch and the side field. All closed. At the bottom of the hill, the pond reflected the ocher glow of twilight.

He turned back toward the cabinet as a cheer went up from the television. If he was sure the doors had been closed when he left the room, not many possibilities were left for how they'd been opened. Gram hadn't moved from her spot at the dining room table. He certainly hadn't had a sudden, quick bout of sleepwalking between sitting on the couch and returning to the room. No one else was in the house.

No one human, anyway.

He rubbed his arms, anger rising as he stared at the cabinet. In his line of work, he dealt with concrete things. Math. Measurements. Timelines. He didn't like what he couldn't control, what he couldn't interpret. He was comfortable with calculations and blueprints, not spirits and cryptic messages from beyond.

His jaw tightened as frustration built. If he was going to believe a ghost did this, what was it supposed to mean? Did the puzzles in the cabinet serve as some sort of clue, an indication that there was a mystery to be solved? Or was this just a sign from Pop—a blatant manipulation of the physical world he could no longer ignore? If that was the case, did Pop just want him to accept that his spirit really was here? Or did the contents of the cabinet still mean something? Gram and Pop used to love doing puzzles together. When he and Ryan were little, the four of them had spent many nights around the dining room table, working together, sharing the excitement of finding a key piece or connection.

He shook his head to clear it. One person could help them with this, and right now, the most important thing was making sure she was safe. Because now he had no choice but to believe the things happening to her were not products of an active imagination or bizarre accidents. She had become a target, possibly due to her abilities. Something here didn't want her around, and he didn't think it was Pop.

Resisting the urge to slam the cabinet doors back into place, he closed them carefully, then dropped onto the couch. He set his beer down and started typing. "Hey, it's Luke. Just checking to see if you're OK?"

His breath came out in a rush of relief as a trio of gray dots came up on the screen—proof Callie was on the other end, crafting a reply. It came a moment later. "Hey! I'm OK. Quiet weekend. Are you all OK? Did something happen?"

He glanced at the cabinet. "We're fine. And not really,

just doors opening etc." As he hit send, he wondered if that was enough for her to guess he was coming around to accept the ghost thing.

"Same here. Bathroom door slamming at 5 am woke me this morning." She punctuated this with a sad face.

His mouth twitched in a small smile. It was incredible that she could make light of this, considering what had happened to her. He tried to picture her at her apartment, which wasn't easy, since he'd never seen it. But her image was easy to conjure. Long, thick hair the color of black coffee, the dark brown contrasting with her light green eyes. A pale dusting of freckles over the bridge of her nose. Full pink lips with the alluring angles of a peaked Cupid's bow along the top. Her lithe, toned body…

He shifted positions as his blood heated, returning his focus to the screen. "That sucks," he responded, unsure where to go from here. He wanted to ask her what she was doing, but that might sound creepy. Might as well just follow up by asking her what she was wearing. He wanted to reiterate Gram's invitation to come stay at Hillwood, but that might sound too forward, coming from him.

He frowned. No other woman he could think of had ever put him in knots like this. His sudden uncertainty was foreign. Then again, the situation was certainly unprecedented.

With a heavy sigh, he added, "Will you come by tomorrow if you have time?" There. Innocuous enough. But he did want to talk to her about everything, now that he had a new outlook on the strange events.

Hell, he wanted to see her, too. May as well admit it to himself.

"Sure. What time?"

"Whatever works for you. I'll be around, working on the barn and my house."

"K."

He inhaled deeply, debating. Then he typed, "Have a good night. Be careful."

"Thanks. You too."

CHAPTER 14

*S*omething tickled her forehead, interrupting her dream. Callie tried to brush it away, but layers of sleep pinned her limbs down. Slumber pulled her back under, heavy and insistent.

She flinched as the sensation disturbed her again. A bead of water dripped onto her face, trickling down her cheek. Another. Cold, wet droplets. A dank smell filled her nostrils.

Her eyes flew open as panic sliced through her. The oxygen left her lungs in a strangled gasp. No! *Oh please God no.*

A figure stood by the side of the bed, bent forward over Callie, its features gray and murky in the darkness. Empty black eye sockets stared down at her as torn lips leered. Tangled strands of dark hair hung down in a sodden curtain, dripping water onto the pillow.

A scream built in Callie's throat, but no sound emerged. Her muscles were locked in ice, useless and immobile.

Only her heart moved, thrashing frantically in her chest like a dying bird.

Another drop splashed the skin beside her nose, and terror broke through her paralysis. Callie cried out, scrambling away from the specter to the other side of the bed. Please don't let it follow me. She pictured it flying toward her with inhuman speed, reaching out with clawed fingers. This time it was going to succeed in killing her. She half-jumped, half-fell out of the bed, watching it as she stumbled into the corner. Now she was trapped.

Something brushed against her ear and she shrieked, batting it away. But the figure on the other side of the bed hadn't moved. It stood in the shadows, its head down. Callie reached a shaking hand up and touched a spiky leaf. Just her hanging spider plant.

And the windows were to her left. They were unlocked, cracked to allow the night air in. Should she yank one all the way open and try to jump? It was only two stories up. But below was an unforgiving paved lot.

The lamp on her dresser registered in her peripheral vision. She'd never wished for light with more desperation than right now. But even if she found the courage to lunge for the lamp, it probably wouldn't work. She'd left the hall light on when she'd gone to bed, and it no longer glowed in the doorway.

Muffled plops fell on the sheets, breaking up the silence. She was going to go mad. Right here, right now. If she survived long enough.

Beneath the windows was a bookshelf, and Callie reached out and grabbed a heavy candle in a thick glass jar from the top shelf. What would happen if she threw it? Would it injure the ghost? Or would it simply anger it, causing it to attack? She drew in a shuddering breath, gripping the improvised weapon with her damp hands. *What do I do?*

No inner voice answered her at first. But then a thought surfaced—she was a psychic. Maybe this thing needed something. Maybe it would leave her alone if it got it. She swallowed hard and tried her voice. "What do you want?" It came out as a rasping plea.

Look what you did. The words crackled in her head, filled with venom, accompanied by a burst of pain. Callie reeled backward, releasing a high-pitched whimper as she squeezed her eyes shut against the agonizing invasion. As she forced them back open, she drew back her arm. The instinct to fight back was too strong to ignore.

It was gone.

The shock brought her momentum to a halt, but the candle still launched, sailing through the air in a small arc before landing on the mattress. It bounced once and settled beside the forgotten flashlight.

Was it hiding behind the bed? Beneath the bed? The image was almost too horrifying to envision—the stuff of nightmares. Leg muscles quaking, she side stepped toward the dresser, sending up a silent prayer as she turned the knob on the lamp.

One click. A second click, and a cone of light illuminated the corner of the room. Her shoulders slumped as a wave of relief crashed over her.

But she still had to check. With each step, dread built,

until her stomach heaved and bile burned her throat. She rounded the bottom corner of the bed, peering around to where the figure had stood. Nothing.

She took a tentative step closer, studying the worn carpet. Every cell in her body recoiled as she stretched her foot toward the spot right next to the bed. Biting hard on her lip, she touched her toe to the dark patch of carpet. Cold. Wet. She snatched her foot away, staggering back.

She swallowed back the acid filling her mouth, sinking slowly to her knees. Tremors vibrated through her hand as she reached for the bed skirt. Holding her breath, she flicked it up, a scream poised on her lips.

Nothing but rolls of wrapping paper and a set of five pound hand weights.

She sagged back on her heels, willing her racing pulse to slow. Okay. Pushing herself up, she retrieved the flashlight from the sheets and plucked her phone off the nightstand. Then she made her way to the kitchen, flicking on every light switch she passed.

Should she bother checking the rest of the apartment? It didn't make much sense, considering the intruder was a ghost who could appear without warning and then vanish into thin air. She sighed, filling a glass of water at the sink. So much for reclaiming her bedroom. She'd felt so good after hearing from Luke. So strong. His concern, the relatively calm weekend, and her aching body had teamed up to make sleeping in her comfortable bed seem like the best course of action.

Would the spirit have shown up anyway, no matter where she slept? It probably made no difference. Still, the couch just felt safer. Plus, she could watch TV, because she was pretty sure sleep wasn't going to be an option after all that. *Look what you did.* The horrible accusation rattled around her brain like shards of bone.

As she sipped her water, she glanced at her cell, contemplating texting Luke. Alice had said to get in touch at any time if she needed help. But honestly, what could he do? It was 3:30 in the morning. He'd probably be up in a few hours; she'd contact him then.

She wandered over to the couch, pulling the blanket off the back of the cushions. One of the decorative pillows would have to work, she decided, wedging the softest one into the armrest. No way was she using the damp pillow from her bed, even with a fresh pillowcase.

With a grimace, she swiped a hand over her face. The water drops had dried, but she still had the sudden pressing urge to wash any traces of that *thing* off her skin. Gathering her flashlight and phone, she trudged to the bathroom.

CHAPTER 15

*S*he sat cross-legged on top of a table, watching Luke work. They were inside the house he was renovating, but he was currently building more saddle racks for the barn. Country rock played softly from a speaker by her knee.

She'd been at Hillwood every day this week so far. When she'd shown up on Monday morning, Alice and Luke had already been filled in on her terrifying middle-of-the-night visitor from her earlier phone call. Alice had immediately swept her up into a comforting hug; to Callie's surprise, Luke had followed suit. As he wrapped her in a protective embrace, the tension in her body seemed to melt away. His strong arms stayed around her long enough for it to feel intimate, and a flush heated Callie's cheeks when they separated.

Together, they'd discussed everything that had happened over the weekend. Alice continued to refresh coffee mugs as they analyzed the new information. It wasn't much. Callie hadn't been able to clearly see the figure's face, due to the darkness, the dripping tangle of hair, and the sheer horror. At least she could be certain it was a woman, though, and that put the disgruntled former farmhand theory to rest. Callie's new theory was that this woman may have died somewhere on the property, which made her spirit stronger than Henry's, despite the fact that he'd lived at Hillwood his entire life. But neither Alice nor Luke could come up with any guesses as to who the mystery woman might be, or why she was currently tormenting them. The one bright spot in the frustration surrounding the mystery was that Luke no longer seemed to have any doubts about the existence of ghosts.

Callie had spent most of that day going through the boxes from the attic, discovering nothing of significance. A peaceful sleep that night gave her renewed energy, though, and on Tuesday morning she returned to Hillwood to continue her task. She and Luke had gone on another trail ride, too. Friday evening's kiss had not come up, even while they were alone in the privacy of the woods. It was as though they'd made an unspoken agreement as they left the barn to keep the conversation light. God knew they both deserved a respite from difficult subjects.

Now it was Wednesday, a bizarre anniversary of sorts. "You know what I realized?" she asked. "It was a week ago today that I first came to Hillwood."

One side of Luke's mouth quirked in a half-smile. "I bet you regret that decision on an hourly basis."

She laughed. "A normal person probably would. But...I wanted to help, and I still do." Glancing away, she threaded her fingers through her hair. "And I'm glad I met you and Alice."

He straightened, giving her a long look. "I'm glad too. But I do worry about you." Exhaling, he set the power drill down on a workbench. "I'm hoping you'll reconsider coming to stay here with us, in the house." Locking his gaze with hers, he added, "I promise not to kiss you unexpectedly again. I just wanted to say that, in case what happened the other night is factoring into your decision."

Oh. Her pulse accelerated. "I...," she trailed off, twisting her hands together. She wanted to be honest with him. And to make sure he knew she'd enjoyed the kiss, even though it couldn't go anywhere. It was time to explain why, before things got complicated. She swallowed hard and tried again. "I liked the kiss. Actually, that's the understatement of the year." If she was going to be honest, she may as well go for broke. "It's just that...well, this is going to sound presumptuous, but it's just that I'm not a person who can have a relationship."

He frowned, his brow creasing. "Why not? Is it the psychic thing?"

She lifted her hair off the back of her neck, hoping to cool the fire spreading through her. "That's part of it."

He took a few steps closer to her, settling his hands on his hips. "What's the rest?"

"It's a sad story."

Pushing himself up onto the table, he sat beside her. "Tell me."

Blowing out a breath, she twisted her hair into a coil over one shoulder. "Okay," she agreed, her voice wavering slightly. "You already know about my parents. My mom and I had to move my dad into a memory care center when I was a junior in college. At that point, he was becoming a danger to himself and to others, but we also knew my mom's prognosis was bad, and there was no way I could manage Dad myself if she was gone. When he first started showing signs, I decided to stay local for college, and live at home to help out. But even leaving him for a few hours here and there to attend classes would have been disastrous."

Luke reached for her hand, sliding his fingers through hers. "I'm sure that must have been a tough decision."

She nodded. "It was. But, I did have someone I relied on, someone who was always there for me." Her throat tightened. "Andrew and I started dating when I was 16. He was the other reason I didn't want to go away to school. My friends thought it was ridiculous, but I knew what we had was real. We were together seven years."

Luke remained silent, his head down, his grip on her hand firm and comforting.

"He helped get me through everything. My dad's decline, my mom's death. We were going to get married. He was saving up for a ring." She inhaled, fighting to stay in control.

"Then one night, there was this concert in Boston I wanted to go to. I was really excited because I managed to get tickets at the last minute. Andrew didn't think we should go, because it was winter and the forecast was calling for some freezing rain later that night. But I convinced him."

Luke seemed to sense where her story was going, and he pulled her hand onto his lap and cupped his other hand around it, enclosing it entirely.

It was getting more difficult to choke out the words, but she had to finish. "A tractor-trailer lost control and hit us. Our car rolled. I don't remember anything beyond that, but I learned later that Andrew died before the rescuers could even get us out."

"Oh, God, Callie. That's awful."

She stifled a sob. "It was my fault."

"No. You couldn't have known what would happen."

Tears welled in her eyes. "That's what Andrew said."

It took Luke a moment to process her meaning. "You... spoke to him? After?"

She wiped at her face with her free hand, nodding her head. "I was in a coma for a few days, but right after the accident, while I was in surgery, I nearly died too. I flat-lined for a few seconds. And the whole 'head towards the light' thing happened to me. It was beautiful, and I wanted to go. And then there was my mother, somehow communicating with me in this place in-between. She wouldn't let me go with her. She told me I had to stay. When I kept trying to get to her, she reminded me that Dad needed me. So, I stayed."

"Wow. That's incredible."

She took the bottle of water he passed to her, pulling in a long sip. "I regretted it, once I woke up and learned about Andrew. I was inconsolable. I didn't want to get out of my hospital bed, I wouldn't eat, I refused to participate in rehab. And then Andrew started talking to me, insisting he

127

loved me and he didn't want me to feel guilty, that it wasn't my fault. I thought it was a result of my head injury. The doctors claimed I was lucky, and that my brain injury was considered mild, but when you keep hearing voices, it's pretty easy to come to the conclusion that you've lost your mind."

"I'm sure."

"But then another spirit started speaking to me, asking me to relay a message to one of my physical therapists, and when the things I suddenly knew from the voices were confirmed by someone else, I realized maybe I wasn't crazy. It was enough to convince me Andrew's spirit really was talking to me. And he told me he couldn't move on until I forgave myself and dedicated all my energy to recovery. So...I did my best. For him. And for my dad. And eventually, once I got stronger, Andrew said goodbye." She closed her eyes, drained.

Still holding her hand, Luke pushed himself off the table and turned to face her. He pulled her towards him, murmuring, "I'm so, so sorry, Callie." As she unfolded her legs and leaned into him, he wrapped his arms around her.

Hot, silent tears slipped down her cheeks as he held her against his chest. Beneath her ear, the sound of his heartbeat calmed her own. Her head moved slightly with the rise and fall of his quiet breaths, the rhythm steady and soothing.

When the pain had ebbed and the tears had dried, she lifted her face to look up at him. "I'm sorry," she said shakily. She pulled one of her hands from around his waist and ran a knuckle beneath her swollen eyes. "I didn't mean to unload all this emotional stuff on you. I just...wanted you to know."

He laid his forehead against hers. "I'm glad you told me. I asked you to, remember?"

She squeezed her eyes shut. "Yes."

"But I agree with Andrew. It was not your fault. Accidents happen."

Pulling in a breath, she opened her eyes. His wide chest filled her field of vision, the dark splotches on his gray T-shirt a reminder of her tears. She hadn't wanted to lose control in front of him. And yet, she felt better.

Luke lifted his head, sliding his hands up to smooth her hair. "Andrew sounds like a great guy who loved you very much. I don't think he would want you to swear off relationships forever."

"He was a great guy. And I have no doubt he would want me to be happy. I just can't risk going through that kind of pain ever again." She paused for a beat. "And I hope you don't think I was implying you might want a relationship with me. I just wanted you to know why I'm...the way I am," she finished, lifting one shoulder in a small shrug.

"Hey." He cupped the sides of her face, gently tipping her head back until their eyes met. "I think you're amazing." His thumbs trailed over her cheekbones in a slow caress. "And I do want you to think about coming to stay here, at least while this scary stuff is going on. If you want me to promise not to kiss you again, I will."

She blinked at him, dazed. "Do you *want* to kiss me again?"

"Yes."

Her heart flipped. Suddenly, all she wanted was to feel his mouth on hers. To forget about everything but this man, standing in front of her, stroking her skin with the rough pads of his thumbs. "I want you to kiss me, too," she said, her voice low and breathless.

He lowered his face to hers, his lips lingering above hers for an agonizing moment of anticipation. She moaned as his mouth closed over hers, and tender kisses quickly turned urgent, like fire gaining fuel.

She slipped her hands under his shirt, running her palms up the hard planes of his back. His lips traveled down to her neck, his stubble lightly scraping her jawline. Oh, God. He gripped her hips, pulling her closer to the edge of the table, and her thighs tightened around his legs. She was nothing but heat and desire now; flesh and nerves.

A thump rattled the front wall, and they broke apart, turning in unison toward the sound. "What was that?" Callie whispered.

"I'm not sure I care." He dipped his head again to nuzzle her neck.

She eased away as coherent thoughts began returning to her muddled mind. God, what was she doing? If she wasn't careful, she was going to fall for him. And what about Luke? If he developed feelings for her, she would only end up hurting him. She'd told him she wasn't relationship material, but did he understand that wasn't going to change?

"We have to check," she insisted, scooting back on the table. She folded one leg in and swiveled, averting her gaze from the evidence of his arousal.

"You're right," he agreed with a sigh, straightening his shirt and tugging at his jeans. He turned, scanning the drywall interior of the front of his house. "It sounded like something hit the window."

She hopped off the table. "Oh, I hope it wasn't a bird." That would be horrible. But she could tell by the sudden tension in the room they both had the same thought: that it could be something far worse than that. Dread pumped through her veins as she followed Luke over to the newly installed window.

Luke looked out the top of the window, his hand resting on her back. "I don't see anything out there."

But her eyes caught on something in the lower sash, and her lungs froze. Two handprints smudged the glass. The marks were faint and smeared, but there was no mistaking the shape. It looked as though someone had slapped their palms against the outside of the window as they peered inside. With enough force to make that sound.

"Luke…," she managed, pointing a trembling finger toward the marks. "It's handprints. From outside."

He crouch down to inspect them. "I see it. Maybe they were already there, though, before I even hung it. Someone could have touched it during manufacturing or shipping."

She knew what he was doing. It was too ingrained in him still, the need to find a rational explanation. "No. You would have noticed. And…the sound."

He nodded as he stood. "You're right."

"That thing was watching us." Her voice cracked with a sob. Oh, God. It was the woman who'd been standing over her. The prints were too small to belong to a man. A shudder tore through her.

"It's okay," he murmured, pulling her into his arms. "We're okay." He held her for a moment, his chin resting on the top of her head.

"Should we check on Alice?"

His jaw slid across her hair as he nodded. "Yeah, I think we'd better."

CHAPTER 16

*L*uke didn't like the way his brother kept touching Callie.

It had taken a lot of convincing, from both Luke and Gram, to get her to agree to come to dinner at Hillwood tonight, since other members of the Turner Family would be here as well. It was just Ryan and their parents, John and Cynthia, but he understood how she might feel awkward. Still, perhaps selfishly, he wanted her there. As did Gram. And so they'd pushed.

The family gathered at least once a month for a Sunday dinner at the farmhouse; it had been a long-standing tradition. Nothing fancy, just a regular opportunity to get together and enjoy good food. This would be the second month without Henry, though, and it was hard for everyone to see his chair at the head of the table left vacant.

Having Callie here would help lighten the mood, and hopefully keep everyone on their best behavior. But it would also give him a break from worrying about her safety. Since the handprints on the glass last Wednesday, only little nuisance things had happened, both here at Hillwood and at Callie's apartment. Or so she claimed, anyway. He knew she was still having trouble with the idea of coming to stay with them; he hoped she wasn't keeping anything from him.

Callie's theory was that maybe Henry was getting stronger, getting better at interfering with the female spirit's malicious actions. That hadn't exactly made him feel better. Personally, he was worried the thing was just recharging its batteries, gearing up for its next big scheme. That made him feel worse. At least, if Callie was with them most of the evening, she'd be around other people. He could keep an eye on her.

Until she went home again. He sighed inwardly, glancing past his father's shoulder to where she was standing with Ryan. He'd had her cornered since he'd arrived, chatting with her over drinks and appetizers while their parents kept Luke busy, asking him question after question on the other side of the living room. This wasn't unusual; they didn't see Luke as much as they saw Ryan. Ryan worked with their dad. What was unusual was his overwhelming desire to get away from them right now, so he could be with Callie.

Gram had excused herself for a minute to check the ham, and when she returned, she announced it was ready. All the other dishes had been made in advance, by Cynthia, Callie, and Gram, and they'd been set out already. Callie had insisted on contributing if she was going to attend, and she'd made the salad. Luke had warned her not to even think about sampling any cherry tomatoes while she put it together. He was pleased she'd left them off entirely, opting instead for a spinach and goat cheese salad with crushed walnuts and dried cranberries.

His eyes narrowed as Ryan settled his hand on Callie's lower back as they all made their way into the dining room. Officially, the story was still that Callie was going to board her imaginary horse "Dragonfly" at Hillwood, and that she and Gram had hit it off as friends. The three of them had decided it wasn't time to disclose the real-life ghost story they'd been living yet. He and Gram had promised Callie they'd jump in if she needed help answering any horse-related questions, but they'd already developed Dragonfly's basic details in what had turned into a humorous conversation.

So, to be fair, Ryan didn't know the status of Luke's relationship with Callie.

Hell, Luke himself didn't know the status of his relationship with Callie. But he recognized what he was feeling: good old fashioned jealousy. He tamped it down. He had no claim on Callie. He wasn't sure he even wanted a claim on her. Those six months with Blair had been more than enough relationship drama to last a lifetime, and only two months had passed since things had finally quieted down.

It didn't take long for his mother to delve into the subject, though. Halfway through the meal, she lifted her wineglass and gestured toward Luke and Callie. The diamonds around Cynthia's wrist flashed beneath the old brass chandelier as she asked, "Now, are you two dating?"

He could sense Callie stiffening in her seat beside him. All eyes were suddenly on them; Gram's blue gaze was especially alert. Great. He needed to deflect the attention away from Callie immediately, before she became uncomfortable. "Oh, um, no. Just friends." *Who kiss on occasion.*

"I'm sure he's a bit gun-shy after the Blair fiasco," Ryan pointed out as he scooped up a forkful of potato salad.

"Please don't mention that name," Cynthia said, her lips pursing as though she'd just bitten into a rotten apple.

For once, he was in complete agreement with his mother, and he was grateful for her response. He'd thought about telling the story when Callie had shared her past, but what he'd gone through felt like a minor nuisance compared to the tragedy Callie endured. He hadn't loved Blair, and she hadn't died.

Callie glanced at him, an inquisitive look on her face. "A clingy ex," he explained. He shot a glare at Ryan before turning to his grandmother. "Gram, can you pass the ham? It's great."

"Just pass me your plate." Alice put down her fork and patted her mouth with her napkin.

He was lifting his plate when a crash from the other side of the house made everyone trade startled looks. Callie's hand gripped his thigh beneath the table, and he quickly set his plate down and covered her hand with his.

"What was that?" asked Cynthia, her groomed eyebrows raised.

Alice flicked a nearly imperceptible glance in his and Callie's direction before offering an exasperated sigh to the rest of the table. "Oh, goodness. One of the barn cats keeps sneaking inside, I bet he knocked something off a shelf."

Cynthia frowned. "You know I'm allergic to cats."

Alice's shoulders stiffened, but she nodded patiently. "Yes, I know. He just showed up here recently, and he seems to want to explore the house, even though I think he knows he's not supposed to be inside."

There was no new cat trying to get inside, at least not that he'd heard about. But it was a plausible explanation; strays and feral cats showed up at the barn on a regular basis. "Maybe he's lost. I'll snap a picture of him and send it into the MSPCA." He did actually do that when he noticed a new feline resident, since cats rarely had collars and sometimes an owner was searching for a lost pet.

"Petey would never have stood for that while he was alive," his Dad said, rising from the table. "I'll go see what it was."

Callie turned to him, her green eyes wide. "Petey?"

He knew what she was thinking. With all the research she'd been doing, she now automatically zeroed in on anyone whose name might fit with the letter written in the flour. And his father had made it clear Petey was no longer alive.

"He was Gram and Pop's dog." He squeezed her hand before releasing it. "Another stray who showed up at the farm a few years ago. The vet guessed he was about eight or nine back then. He just passed away in April." Only a few weeks after Pop's death. He didn't say it out loud, but the momentary silence told him everyone was thinking

137

about it. His gaze slid over to the empty chair at the head of the table.

Callie's face fell. "Oh, I'm so sorry."

"It's okay," Ryan said kindly. "He had a great dog life, at least while we had him. Like Dad said, he loved chasing the barn cats. He never hurt them, he just loved to chase them. And anything that ran, really. Squirrels. Skunks. That ended badly for Petey a few times."

The mood lightened as everyone laughed, and their dad rejoined the table. "A picture fell off a shelf," John said, scooting his chair in. "No sign of a rogue cat."

"I'll look around for him later." He passed his plate to Gram as she motioned with her hands. Clearly she hadn't forgotten he'd requested more ham before. "If all else fails, I'll open a can of tuna." It was interesting how easy the lies about the fake cat came. He knew very well one of the ghosts had knocked the picture over. So did Callie and Gram.

Sure enough, Callie couldn't help herself. "That's a great idea," she said, flashing him a bright smile full of feigned innocence. God, how he loved that she managed to hang on to her sense of humor, even during these strange and scary times.

Miraculously, they got through dinner without any more stressful topics coming up. When Callie made to leave, Luke made sure his body language informed his brother in no uncertain terms that he would be the one walking her out.

He followed her along the porch, around the corner of the house toward the garage, threading his fingers through hers once they'd passed all the living room windows. Her hand was soft and warm, and his body reacted to the connection of their skin in the way he'd come to accept as the new normal: a surge of desire, the need for more. Their shoulders touched as they descended the steps down to the parking area. Lights burned down at the barn; he still had to do the night feeding.

Cars sat in a row across from the garage doors, lined up as though taking in the view of the pond. When they reached her sedan, he pulled her toward him, catching her around the waist with his free hand. "Stay."

The corners of her mouth turned up, but her smile appeared wistful in the shadows. "I should get home. I've intruded on your family time enough for one night."

"No, I mean...stay the night." He lifted their joined hands, rotating their wrists so their palms pressed together.

She gave a soft laugh. "I can't. I don't have any of my things."

He bent his head, grazing her cheek with his nose. "I think we can work around that."

"I'm sure you do," she murmured, a small moan escaping as he nuzzled her ear.

"My plan wouldn't even require pajamas."

"Stop." She giggled, pushing at his shoulder ineffectually. "What are we going to do, wish Alice a goodnight as we stroll up the stairs together?"

He shrugged. "I get the distinct feeling Gram is rooting for us to get together."

"Yeah, me too. Still..."

Her words trailed off as he captured her lips in a passionate kiss, and her hand curled around the back of his neck. He tightened his grip, pulling their bodies closer, savoring the taste of her, the feel of her. A scorching need built inside him at an alarming rate, and he gently broke the kiss before he reached the point where stopping would require a nearly impossible level of control.

Their breaths mingled in ragged gasps. "Seriously," he said, once he'd regained the power of speech. "Please stay. In one of the guest rooms, I mean. I just want you to be safe."

She shook her head. "I know. But I'm not going to let a ghost run my life. I've been okay so far."

A bank of clouds drifted over the silver slice of moon, obscuring the faint glow like an ominous sign from above. Unease washed over him, and he fought the urge to grab her keys as she dug them out of her pocket.

"I'll keep my cell beside me all night. Promise you'll call me immediately if anything happens."

"Promise. You too, okay?"

He promised as well, although they both knew the malevolent spirit seemed focused on Callie now, for what-ever reason. Even though this had all started before Callie even came to Hillwood, she had become a target; she surmised it was due to her abilities. He didn't care about the reasons as much as he cared about protecting her, but he was in uncharted territory here. How could he fight a ghost? He unclenched his fists and opened the car door, kissing her hard before she settled into the driver's seat.

He knew he was going to sound like an overprotective

parent, but he couldn't help himself. "Let me know when you get home, okay?"

Flashing him a smile, she nodded and started up the ignition. Music blared as she fumbled for the volume. "Thanks again for dinner. I have to go take care of my horse Dragonfly now," she added with a wink.

He chuckled despite the trepidation rippling through his nerves. "Drive safe." He eased the door shut and strode back toward the house to allow her room to back out. She lifted her hand in a wave as she pulled away, and he returned the gesture, watching the red taillights curve down the driveway and vanish into the night.

$\mathcal{I}$n the dream, a cold finger tapped her arm, a soft but insistent touch. Scenes shifted through her sleeping mind as she burrowed deeper into the couch. A campfire. Marshmallows. Her parents.

Another series of taps penetrated the layers of slumber, and consciousness began flooding back in. An acrid odor filled her nostrils as a command rang out in her head. *Wake up!* Pressure flared between her temples. A high-pitched hiss drowned out the pleading voice. This was not part of the dream. Her eyes snapped open.

The lights she'd left on were now off, and she bolted upright, pressing her back into the corner of the couch. No filmy apparition stood before her, but an eerie glow cast flickering shadows through the darkness.

Smoke bit into her lungs as she sucked in a breath. Fire! Orange flames leapt from the stovetop in the kitchen, and she clapped a hand over her mouth, staring in stunned silence as her thoughts reeled. The burners had been off;

she hadn't even used them today. And why wasn't the smoke detector working?

This is what the ghost had been gearing up for. And the other one—Henry—had tried to warn her. She scrambled off the couch, taking a few tentative steps toward the kitchen. A roll of paper towels blazed on top of a lit burner, forming a bridge of flames leading to the counter beside the stove.

Piercing beeps split the silence as the smoke detector behind the closed door of her bedroom came to life. Her heart seized before resuming its frantic hammering. She clutched at her chest, coughing. Should she try to put it out? There was a fire extinguisher beneath the sink, but she didn't want to walk through the narrow kitchen to get to it. She didn't want to get that close to the fire, and she wasn't even sure she would know how to work it.

Her horrified gaze fell on the bottle of oil she'd left on the counter after preparing the salad earlier. Flames licked at the plastic container. *Get out. Now!*

But something else tugged her forward. She needed to run to the bedroom, to save the Dragonfly books. She could make it. As she took a step toward the little hallway, her foot landed on a cold, hard object.

Snatching her foot away, she glanced down at the floor. In the firelight, she could see what it was—a battery. Snapping her head back, she confirmed what she already knew: the battery compartment in the smoke detector was open. And empty.

A fresh wave of terror crashed over her, clearing her mind like a slap to the face. She couldn't risk going for the books, not with what this ghost was capable of. Whirling around, she snatched her keys and phone from the table by the couch and dialed 911. She flung open the door, unable to look away from the growing blaze as she breathlessly relayed her emergency.

It was 4:30 a.m. when the firefighters allowed her back into the apartment to collect some personal items. Since the fire had not spread from her kitchen, the other tenants were allowed to return to their units; she'd woken many of them up herself with frantic knocks on neighboring doors while the engines were on their way. Now, she tried to avoid their annoyed glances as they trudged back inside. It hadn't taken long for word to spread that she'd left a burner on. What else could she say? And while a few kind souls had asked about her welfare, the majority of her exhausted neighbors appeared to have less empathy. She couldn't blame them.

The feeble story she'd come up with was that she'd been woken by the sporadic beeps signaling the smoke alarm battery in the kitchen needed to be changed. Once she'd stopped the noise by removing the battery, she'd decided to make some warm milk to help her go back to sleep. Somehow, while trying to do too many things at once in the middle of the night, she'd knocked a roll of paper towels onto the open flame while locating a pot. It was the best she could do beyond telling the truth, which would likely get her thrown in a mental institution.

With a sigh, she tossed clothing and the Dragonfly books—which were thankfully unharmed—into a suitcase. The landlord had informed her she'd have to move out for at least the next month, while the kitchen was restored. He'd been none too happy about the damage, and he hadn't even seen the missing mirror in her bedroom yet. Hopefully some combination of her renter's insurance and his property insurance would pay for the bulk of the repairs. It was too overwhelming to think about right now, but at least she had a place she could stay, for a few nights anyway, while she figured out what to do next. Assuming the invitation was still open.

By the time she'd collapsed into the driver's seat of her car, it was after 5:00 in the morning, and golden pink light streaked the sky. She agonized over calling Hillwood now or waiting another hour. On the one hand, Luke and Alice were probably going to be angry she hadn't called immediately after dialing 911. But on the other was the fact that if they were already going to admonish her for waiting, what difference did it make if she gave them a little more sleep before dropping her latest bombshell?

She scrolled through her meager contact list until she arrived at the two Turner entries. Hesitating for a moment, she pressed Luke's number, unable to explain—even to herself—why she chose him over Alice. She'd never even spoken to him on the phone; they'd only exchanged texts.

He answered on the second ring. "Callie? What's wrong?"

Clearly, an early morning phone call from her was enough to set off alarm bells. "Hey. Um…there was a fire."

Her voice wavered, and she pulled in a deep breath. She was not going to cry.

"What? Are you okay?"

"Yes. But my apartment's not. I can't stay there."

"Oh my God. Okay, where are you? I'm coming to get you."

A dull ache flared through her fingers, and she struggled to relax her death grip on the phone. "No, no. I'm sitting in my car right now. I can drive. I just wanted to make sure…" she trailed off, closing her eyes.

"You're staying here," he said firmly. "Are you sure you don't want me to come pick you up? We can get your car later."

"No, it's fine. I'll be there soon."

"Okay, just drive safely." After a pause, he added, "Just to be clear, the fire…it wasn't an accident, right?"

"No."

He swore under his breath. "I'll go take care of the horses and fill Gram in. See you soon. Be careful, Callie. Please."

His tone radiated concern, and she swallowed hard before she said goodbye. Before she turned the car on, she brought up a playlist of soothing instrumental music she used for cool-downs in her fitness classes. Focusing on the road, she made her way to Hillwood, driving slowly enough to draw the ire of a few early morning commuters.

Once she was settled in the farmhouse kitchen, with a warm drink in her hand and matching pairs of anxious blue eyes trained on her face, she recounted the whole story. As she finished, she circled back to the beginning, to the prodding and the plea that had awoken her when the disabled smoke detector hadn't. "Henry was there, fighting to warn me. I wish he were able to get through to me without her interference. Maybe soon, while she's worn out from last night."

"He can do it," said Alice solemnly. "Right, Henry?" She directed the question into the air above them. Looking back at Callie, she added, "It might be easier with you here all the time, too."

Callie bit down on her lip. "I thought of that. But I feel like I'm bringing danger with me."

"Nonsense. We brought this to *you*." Alice's voice rang with conviction.

Beside her, Luke nodded, his forearms resting on the counter. Rigid tendons shifted beneath his tanned skin as he pushed his fist into his other hand.

She lifted the mug to her lips, letting the steam bathe her face. Alice had made her something called a hot toddy, refusing to give her anything caffeinated. She inhaled the scent of honey and lemon as she sipped, wincing slightly at the sharp tang of whiskey. "But…maybe if I just stayed away from Hillwood for a while, things would calm down."

"No," said Luke, shaking his head. "It won't work. Things were escalating before you came. At this point, I think we need to stick together until we figure this out." He dragged his fingers through his hair. "I can't believe I'm saying this, but is there anything else we could try? Ouija boards? A séance? Or…maybe an exorcism?"

"Well, I've never tried the first two things. To be honest, I've never needed to, and I'm not sure it would make it any easier to connect, but I'm not opposed to trying. I'm pretty sure exorcisms are reserved for demons, though, and I don't think she's a demon."

"Close enough."

Incredibly, a tiny chuckle came out in the same breath as a sigh. "You're right. At least in terms of the horrible things that have been happening to us. But I think we'd have trouble convincing the Catholic Church or whoever it is in charge of exorcisms these days. What we have is an angry, violent, vengeful ghost...but she must want something beyond just causing chaos and fear. We just have to figure out what that is so we can put her to rest."

Alice cut in. "Speaking of rest, I think it's time for you to try to get some sleep, Callie. You must be exhausted."

She blinked, suddenly noticing how heavy her eyelids had grown. The whiskey burned pleasantly in her chest, flowing through her veins and loosening her muscles. Things were shutting down in her sleep-deprived mind, like lights in department stores blinking off as the mall prepared to close for the night. She bobbed her head in a nod.

"Okay, let's get you upstairs," Alice commanded in her take-charge voice. "I'm going to get you settled and then start washing your clothes, because no offense, but they're a little smoky." She barreled on before Callie could interrupt, holding out her palm. "No arguments. I'll take what you're wearing and what you've packed and it will be done by the time you wake up. I'll get you one of Luke's shirts to sleep in."

She nearly melted at the thought of snuggling into a

comfortable bed, wearing Luke's clothing, but fear pricked at her with persistent jabs. "But...will you two be safe?"

Luke caught her around the waist, helping her off the stool. "We'll be fine. Gram and I will keep an eye on each other while you're asleep. I'm going to set up some precautions, too. I'll double check the smoke detectors, and I can do a few things to make it harder to start a fire around here. Turn off the gas supply at night, move everything far away from burners, double-check electrical wiring."

"Okay." It was all she could manage as she followed them through the dining room. Maybe taking preventative action would help. A ghost could only do so much in the physical world—of this, she was certain, because otherwise the vicious spirit would have certainly strangled her to death by now. So if they made manipulating objects around here more difficult, they might be able to thwart a future attack.

Unless the ghost came up with something they didn't think of in advance. An icy shiver slithered up her spine as she climbed the stairs.

CHAPTER 18

She slept until a little after noon, and then ate blueberry pancakes and sausage nearly as fast as Alice could slide them off the griddle. After coffee, she helped Alice clean up the kitchen and do some other household chores while Luke caught up with paperwork. The three of them went on a trail ride together, taking Sasha, Lady, and Diablo, a striking black horse who turned out to be a lot sweeter than his name suggested. Determined to stay in a group as much as possible, they lugged one of the boxes from the attic down to Luke's house, so he could get some work done on the renovation while Alice and Callie read through old documents. Thankfully, she'd found coverage for her classes for the next several nights, so she didn't have to go anywhere on her own.

After dinner, they watched a movie, and Luke convinced Alice and Callie to start getting ready for bed while he took care of the horses for the night. Callie stared at her cellphone screen as she filled the old tub, refusing to slip into the warm water until he'd returned to the house and called up that everything was okay.

The routine of a bath before bed felt slightly awkward in someone else's home, but she decided she'd better get used to it if she was going to be staying here for a while. She'd stumbled through a quick shower this morning before lying down, just to get the smoke smell out of her hair. Now, though, she wanted to soak and hopefully unwind—as much as possible anyway, given the circumstances. The old claw foot tub in the hall bathroom was quaint and welcoming, and she felt some of the tension of the last 24 hours seeping out from her body into the warm, fragrant water with each luxurious minute. After she climbed out and dried off, she stood in front of the fogged mirror, sliding a comb through her wet hair. A little knot of anxiety returned as she braced herself for a wispy figure to appear behind her, or for an unseen finger to slash words into the steamy glass. But only her reflection stared back at her, and she breathed a sigh of relief when she opened the door to the bathroom and turned out the lights.

Wrapped in a towel, she padded toward her new bedroom, the wood floor of the hallway groaning softly beneath her footsteps. The chilled air that greeted her when she entered was from the rattling AC unit lodged in the window, not a supernatural presence, and she sighed gratefully even as she hurried across the room to shut it off. She'd turned it on earlier to cool the room down, but now it was a little much in her current state of undress.

When she turned around, Luke was standing in the doorway. "Oh!" she gasped, her pulse jumping. She'd forgotten to close the door. One of the hazards of living alone for so long.

"Sorry, Callie. I didn't mean to sneak up on you."

"It's okay. I guess I didn't hear you, with the AC on." She gestured toward the window with her head, suddenly acutely aware she was clad in only a towel.

He nodded, pushing his hands into his pockets. "How was your bath?"

"Good, thanks. I was hoping it would help me relax." She shrugged, and the twist in her towel loosened. Clutching it to her chest, she managed a weak smile as she fumbled to secure it. She could feel the weight of his stare even as she bent her head to check the new knot, and warmth pooled in her belly.

"And did it?" he asked, his voice low.

"What?" She glanced up, and their gazes locked. The air crackled as the moment stretched out, and she recognized something in the depths of his eyes. *Hunger.* Could he see the same thing reflected back in hers?

His chest expanded as he pulled in a slow breath. "Did it help relax you?"

"Oh. Um, a little." Desire burned through her, deep and insistent, and she suddenly wanted nothing more than to lose herself in his arms. To forget everything else in the world except for Luke. To forget fear and loss; to leave no room for anything but pleasure.

"Well, I just wanted to check in on you. To see if you... need anything."

Yes. I need you. The bold words caught in her throat, and she licked her lips and tried a different response. "Do you?"

He cocked his head, his brows pulling together. "What?"

"Um. Need anything?"

He dragged a hand over his mouth, the muscles in his arm bunching with the movement. "That's a dangerous question to ask when you're standing there in a towel."

A loaded silence hung between them, heavy with possibilities. Her voice trembled slightly when she finally broke it. "And yet I'm asking it."

He entered the room slowly, shutting the door behind him with a soft click. "Are you sure about this?"

She swallowed. *Was she?* Her body certainly was. Every inch of her skin tingled, craving his touch. "Yes. I'm sure."

He closed the distance between them in three quick strides, grasping the sides of her face with his hands. Tilting her head back, he anchored her in place as his lips crushed hers in a demanding kiss. The rough pads of his thumbs slid over her cheeks, and a groan rumbled in his chest.

She strained up to him, lifting to her toes, grabbing onto his shoulders. The hard muscles tightened beneath her touch. Heat flooded her veins, her heartbeat thundered in her ears. *Luke.*

The scruff of his stubble scraped against her cheek as his mouth moved across her jaw. He caught the tender lobe of her ear in his teeth, and she moaned.

He stilled, pulling away from her slightly. Their breath mingled, rasping and urgent, as he dropped his forehead to hers. "Callie," he said, his voice low and jagged.

"What is it? What's wrong?"

He sighed, cursing under his breath. "You've been

through a lot. I want you here so I can keep you safe. I shouldn't be taking advantage of the situation."

"You're not," she whispered. "This is what I want. What I need. All that matters is this moment, and right now, I need you." She twined her fingers into the hair at the nape of his neck, pressing herself against him.

"You're sure?"

In answer, she nuzzled his neck, trailing kisses up to his jawline. She didn't want to think about the past, she didn't want to think about the future, she didn't want to think about all the eerie events plaguing their lives. She didn't want a single thought left in her mind; she wanted only sensation and release. Kissing Luke made reality fade away...falling into bed with him would make it vanish completely.

"I'm taking that as a yes," he managed as he captured her mouth in another intoxicating kiss. His fingers trailed over her collarbone, catching on the twisted knot of terrycloth.

"Yes," she murmured.

The towel slid down her body, falling to the floor.

CHAPTER 19

*S*he drifted on the edge of consciousness, awareness seeping in slowly as sunlight played over her closed eyelids. This wasn't the couch. Not her bed, either. Her limbs were heavy, her muscles unresponsive. Where was she? Oh, yes…in Alice's guestroom. She shifted, stretching her legs beneath the sheets.

"Good morning, beautiful."

Oh my God. Her eyes flew open as memories flooded in. She and Luke…

He curled an arm around her, pulling her back into his chest. "I've been patiently waiting to do this," he said, nuzzling her neck. "I didn't want to wake you up."

She was speechless for a moment as her body responded to his touch. Last night had been…amazing. Beyond amazing. But now, reality was setting in. Here she was, a guest in Alice's house for one night, and she was lying naked in bed with her hostess's grandson. Oh, God. Had Alice realized Luke was in here, with her? She squeezed her eyes shut and fought the urge to succumb to the desire coursing through her veins again. Turning toward him, she pressed a palm into his shoulder. "What time is it? Is Alice awake?"

He gave her a playful frown. "Is that your version of good morning?"

This time she swatted him.

"Fine." Capturing her hand, he twined their fingers as he heaved a dramatic sigh. "Let's see. It's probably about 6:30. I need to get down to the barn, but I didn't want to wake you. And I think Gram is up, I heard her go downstairs."

"Does she know?"

His brow furrowed in feigned confusion. "Know what?"

"Stop," she insisted, using the sternest tone she could manage without raising her voice. She was unable to keep a smile from curving her lips, though.

"Well, I got up in the middle of the night and shut my bedroom door, so she wouldn't worry if she woke up before me, saw I wasn't in there, and then couldn't find me. So she probably doesn't know we're in bed together at the moment." Beneath the sheets, he slid his leg over hers. "But it's not a big deal. She knows I date."

Now it was her turn. She arranged her features in surprised innocence. "Was this a date?"

"It was a great date," he said, grinning as he rolled on top of her. He held himself above her, pinning her hand by her head. His expression turned serious as he held her gaze. "Truthfully, though, I was afraid if I used the term 'relationships', you'd freak out."

She closed her eyes and nodded, her hair sliding against the pillow. *He knew her.*

"Hey," he murmured, pressing his lips against her forehead. "It's okay. I'm scared, too. But we don't have to define this to anyone. Not even to ourselves." He trailed kisses across her cheek and along her jawline, his free hand slipping beneath the sheets.

Her breath caught as his mouth brushed the tender skin of her neck. She squirmed beneath him, arching her back as pressure built with devastating intensity.

He kissed the corner of her mouth. "Am I allowed to say I care about you?"

"Mmm," she managed, digging her nails into the solid muscles of his shoulders.

"Am I allowed to say I find you irresistible?" he continued, relentless.

A moan escaped between his kisses. "I thought you said you had to go feed the horses," she teased, even as she pulled him closer, desperate to eliminate even the tiniest bit of space between their bodies.

"They can wait a little longer."

"I'LL BE upstairs for a while, then," Alice added, after coming out onto the porch to announce she was going to take an afternoon nap. She gave them both a broad smile, her eyes crinkling in what could have been a wink, before going back inside the house. The screen door slapped lightly in her wake.

Callie waited for Alice's footsteps to fade up the stairs before twisting in her chair toward Luke. "She knows." The words came out in a cross between a hiss and a whisper.

He shrugged, sliding his gaze away from the fields beyond the porch railing. "Maybe."

A thread of anxiety wound through her. "Did you say something?"

Reaching over, he clasped her hand, linking their fingers on top of the wide wooden armrest. "I think she's just reading our body language. We've both probably seemed a bit...content this morning," he said with a roguish grin. When she didn't return the smile, he squeezed her hand. "It's fine, really. I think we all have bigger problems to worry about."

It was true, and his comment jiggled something in her brain. Something that had tried to present itself this morning while they were in bed, before he'd erased all coherent thoughts. "What happened with Blair?"

His expression turned dark, the surprise registering in his eyes. "What?"

"Blair. You said she was your ex, right? And earlier this morning, you suggested you've had relationship issues in the past, too. So what happened?"

He sighed, rubbing the back of his neck with his free hand. "Yeah, she's my ex. We were together for about six months, and she was..." Clearing his throat, he started again. "She was mentally unstable, I guess you could say. Things ended badly."

Her heartrate accelerated, and she pulled her hand away. "What do you mean, badly?"

A deep crease formed between his brows. "Callie, there is absolutely nothing between me and her now."

She shook her head. "But…how did it end?"

"Like I said, she had some serious problems. Depression, addiction, jealousy. She was…I guess you could say she was stalking me, at the end. Coming to my house, my work, the law office, here. Telling me lies, like pretending her mother had died to gain sympathy. I had to threaten to get a restraining order to make it stop."

The word 'jealousy' rattled through her head, and her blood went cold. "And…that made her stop?"

"Yes, finally."

She stood up, pacing across the weathered planks of the porch. "How do you know?"

"What do you mean?"

Leaning against the railing, she chewed her lip as she gathered her thoughts. "Luke, your family mentioned her the other night at dinner, and a picture fell down. You're saying she was obsessed with you, and this ghost—this *female* ghost—hates me. Her name begins with a 'B', and while it didn't occur to me before, I'm seeing it now. The unfinished letter in the flour…it could have been a capital 'B'."

Silence stretched out as his gaze focused on something in the distance. Shaking his head, he dragged his hands over his face before looking up to meet her eyes. "But she's not dead."

"And you know this for sure? One hundred percent?" Her muscles tightened, her fingers gripping the wooden rail behind her.

He pressed his lips together. "Apparently, she took off. Her roommate got in touch with me, because she was upset about the unpaid bills. The roommate called her mother, too, and her mom said this wasn't unusual behavior, that sometimes she would just get in her car and drive away, without letting anyone know."

A wave of dizziness washed over her. "So no one really knows where she is."

"I guess not." Some of the color drained from his face.

"Did…" She squeezed her eyes shut as an image of the terrifying figure standing over her bed flashed through her mind. "Did she…have long hair?"

"Yes."

"Oh, my God. We need to find out if anyone's heard from her. Right away. Do you still have her mom's number?"

"I can find it."

CHAPTER 20

*I*t didn't take long for Luke to find the number, since he'd called it just a few months ago, when he began to suspect Blair was lying about her mother's death. As Luke spoke into the phone, Callie walked restless circles through the house, from the doorway to the office, through the living and dining rooms and the kitchen, returning to the back hallway where doors also led to the garage and the laundry room. On one pass, she paused at a shelf in the living room, studying some of the family pictures. The glass in Luke's parents' wedding photo had a crack in the corner, and she wondered if that was the frame that fell the other night at dinner. If Blair was the culprit, was she expressing her anger over the derisive way the Turner family was speaking about her? Or had it been Henry, sending a warning? A message to his family, that Blair was the other—threatening—presence in the house? Did Henry know how to stop her? Please, Henry, help me, she pleaded silently, closing her eyes. She braced herself for the stabbing pressure associated with a connection, and the hissing static that would likely block any message from Henry, but nothing came.

Luke approached her as he finished up the phone call, leading her over to the couch. She angled herself into the corner, her foot still bouncing with the need to move.

Rubbing his temples, he pulled in a breath. "Mrs. Adams hasn't spoken to her daughter in years, so she doesn't know very much. The roommate had called, like I mentioned, saying Blair disappeared and looking for some rent and utility money. She said Blair left a lot of things in their apartment, but she did take her purse, her keys, her phone, her car. It wasn't the first time she'd taken off, which is why no one reported her missing. Plus, she's an adult. It's her right to go missing if she wants," he finished with a shrug.

Nausea bubbled in her throat. "She must be dead. Maybe she had an accident."

"No one's reported finding anything, at least according to Mrs. Adams. They would have contacted her if they found an accident scene. But I did call my Dad right after I talked to her. He has some friends who can do extensive searches on people and get much more info than we could online. He was very concerned about why I was asking for help researching Blair, though. He and my mom were not fans."

"I can imagine." She tapped her fingers against her thigh. "Did you tell him why you were asking?"

He shook his head. "Not yet. I wanted to talk to you and Gram first, and I certainly can't imagine telling them Hillwood is haunted over the phone. Once I talk to Gram, maybe I'll see if they can come over tomorrow evening so we can talk."

"Maybe it's time we told them. If Alice agrees, that is." She chewed on her bottom lip, trying to organize her spiraling thoughts. "If Blair is dead, why did she come here to start trouble? She was here before I even met you all. Henry warned me of the danger the first day I came to Hillwood."

"She wasn't a stable person when she was alive. There's no reason to believe her ghost would be any different. When I ended it, she went completely off the rails. She probably still harbors a lot of anger aimed at me. Maybe my family, too. They all had some choice words for her when she tried to contact them to stay connected to me."

A violent shudder rattled through her. "God. That sounds horrible. No wonder she's turned most of her aggression toward me. But, still...there has to be a way to stop this. If her body is out there somewhere, at the bottom of a ravine or something, we have to find her. Give her a proper burial."

"That sounds...challenging."

"That's where I come in. Maybe Henry knows, and he can help."

His jaw tightened. "I don't know, Callie. If it's Blair, and she's after you because she's jealous, maybe it would be best if you just...walk away."

"You want me to go?"

Anguish clouded his features. "Of course not. The selfish part of me wants to be around you all the time. But I don't want anything to happen to you, especially if I can stop it."

"It's too late, though. She's shown us she can follow me. And she was already a dangerous presence before I came on the scene, remember? Henry was worried she'd hurt you or Alice. And she gains strength every day that passes. I'm not leaving until this is finished. Maybe this is my chance to actually save the people I...people I care about." She glanced down at the faded fabric of the couch, startled by her near-admission. *The people I love.* It was true. She loved both Luke and Alice. A steel fist closed around her heart. How had she let this happen? Loving people led to pain.

He reached over, wrapping his hands around her twisting fingers. "None of the things that happened in your past are your fault, Callie. You don't need to redeem yourself."

I do. Out loud, she said, "I'm not leaving. I *will* stop this thing from hurting the people I care about." Even if it came at the expense of her own life. And if she succeeded, she would also be putting a troubled spirit to rest. It wouldn't change what had happened to Andrew, but it was something.

A shrill ring pierced the silence, and they both started. Luke's phone lit up on the coffee table. He peered over, picking it up. "And that's my mom. Right on cue. Clearly my dad told her I'm asking about Blair, and now she's probably in panic mode." With a heavy sigh, he slid his thumb across the screen. "Hey, Mom."

CHAPTER 21

$\mathcal{L}$uke had suggested, quite vocally, that she find a substitute for her Wednesday night class. But she needed the exercise. She needed the money. And she needed to get away from Hillwood for a few hours. She'd assured him she'd be okay—she'd be surrounded by people at the gym. Even while she drove, there would be lots of other motorists around. It sounded right, even though she knew she couldn't make any guarantees. But the other option was just putting her entire life on hold until this was done.

He'd walked her out to her car, then kissed her as though she were leaving for a month before he'd turned back to the house. His parents would be over soon. Truthfully, she was glad she'd miss at least the first part of this visit. She didn't feel like hearing the whole 'can't you see she's a scam artist' conversation again.

She started the car, buckling her seatbelt as she wrinkled her nose. It had been days since she'd driven her car, and a dank musty odor mingled with the faint smell of smoke. With a frown, she glanced at the windows, to see if she'd left one down. But it hadn't rained since Sunday night, had it? She reached over and touched the cloth cover of her passenger seat.

A sudden chill filled the interior of the car, and she stilled, her heart leaping to her throat. Something rustled behind her, and the back of her neck prickled with an awful sense of being watched. Her hand trembled on the gearshift as she slowly lifted her eyes to the rearview mirror.

The horrible, dripping figure slumped in the backseat. Blair. Her head hung down, face hidden by ropes of tangled, wet hair. A sickening giggle floated through Callie's head, and she opened her mouth to scream. Nothing came out; her vocal chords were paralyzed by fear, like in a nightmare.

Get out, a voice screamed in her head, and this was her own voice. But before she could force her frozen muscles to obey the command, the gearshift tore from her grip, ramming itself into Drive. Callie's foot flew off the brake pedal, shoved by an unseen force, as the gas pedal depressed on its own, sending the car lurching forward onto the grass beyond the pavement.

The scream finally emerged, ringing in her ears, as the car gathered speed, hurtling down the hill toward the pond. Panic seized her, clawing at her chest, and she fought to regain control of the car. She stomped futilely at the brakes, but the pedal refused to move at all beneath her foot. Through the windshield, the water raced closer, and she gave up on the brakes, grabbing the handle to her door. She yanked on it, intending to throw herself out of the bouncing vehicle, but the handle wouldn't budge. "No!" she sobbed, unable to stop the mind-numbing terror from taking over. There was no escape; she was trapped. Time stretched out and contracted. She grabbed onto the steering wheel as the car careened down the final expanse of the steep hill and launched into the pond.

A wave of water crashed against the windshield. Her head snapped forward with the impact, the seatbelt driving the breath from her lungs as it locked her body against the seat. Groaning, she worked at the seatbelt clasp with shaking fingers, trying to focus. The car floated along the surface, but the weight of the engine was already pulling the front down. She had seconds to escape. Despair coursed through her veins, mixing with the crushing panic. Even if she could force her mind to tell her what to do and her limbs to cooperate, would Blair let her out?

Don't look. Don't look don't look don't look. But she had to see what she was up against.

The figure remained in the backseat, silent and motionless, only slices of a pale face visible beneath the dark curtain of snarled hair. Tattered light blue fabric clung to dead flesh nearly the same color. One arm was now raised, frozen in place, wrist bent down, skeletal gray fingers curled into a rigid claw.

Oh, God. Bile burned her throat as her stomach heaved, and she tore her gaze away from the horrific specter behind her. Water poured into the car, cold and swift. She had to get out. Scrabbling for the door handle, she yanked on it again, and this time the handle moved in her hand. The rush of relief was quickly tempered by the door's resistance to her frantic shoves, and she realized that her efforts were pointless, even without a ghost interfering. The water pressure outside was too great; the door would not open until the car was completely submerged.

The image of the car sinking, with her inside it, drained the blood from her head, but the shock of the cold water soaking through her clothes, rising higher by the second, kept her conscious. Think! Mouthing a prayer, she jabbed at the window buttons, but the controls refused to work. She beat her palm against the driver's side window in a frantic attempt to break it, barely registering the pain jolting up her arm with each strike. Water climbed up her chest as the car sank lower. Outside, beyond the glass, the evening sunlight glinted on the pond's surface. The bright scene didn't make sense in the context of this macabre nightmare.

She was trapped. Desperation tightened her chest like a vise. "Please!" she cried, aiming her plea over her shoulder. "I know who you are. Blair." The name tasted vile on her tongue, but she tried to keep her message calm despite the tremors in her voice. "Just tell me what you want! Maybe I can help you."

Look what you did.

"I didn't do anything! I never even knew you! Please, just tell me where you are, and we'll find you."

Another soft giggle. *I'm here. And now you are, too.*

Her last thread of control broke, and a primal sob tore

from her throat. The car was nearly under now, the water licking at her neck. She was going to die.

Get ready, a voice in her head commanded. A different voice, deeper and masculine. Bursts of pain, accompanied by static, immediately followed the words, and she suddenly understood. Henry!

A tiny bud of hope bloomed as she fought to decipher his words. Surely Luke's kind Pop wasn't telling her to get ready to die. He was here to help. Would he be strong enough?

And then there was no more time to think. She titled her head back as the water rose over her neck. Grabbing onto the door handle, she pulled in one last breath, filling her lungs as the pond claimed the car.

Time slowed as the steel coffin sank below the surface. The rapid thump of her heartbeat echoed in her ears. Water stung her eyes as she stared down through the windshield and waited—prayed—for Henry's voice to return. Shafts of sunlight pierced the water, revealing the hint of a shadowy object below.

Go! Henry's voice ordered.

Oh, please, she begged silently, as she tried the handle. It moved, pulling forward in her hand. She threw her strength into pushing at the door, fighting against the dark haze of visceral fear threatening to take over. The door opened into the water, and relief surged through her. An angry wail, vibrating with frustration, filled her head as she grabbed onto the doorframe and propelled her body out of the car.

Up. She needed to swim up. Her lungs screamed for air,

and she struggled against the primal urge to breathe. As her legs slid free, she prepared to push off the car with her feet.

An icy claw latched onto her ankle. No! With her free leg, she kicked wildly, twisting and thrashing as pressure built in her chest. Blood pounded in her skull, and she knew she was going to have to give in and allow her lungs to inhale the water. Let me go! Please, Henry, help me. One last time.

Her flailing arms hit something solid, and another hand encircled her wrist, this one warm and strong. Pulling her up, trying to free her from the captive grip below. Tilting her head back, she struggled to focus through the foggy blur of her fading vision.

Luke! Somehow, Luke was here. She allowed him to catch her other arm as she resumed her internal chant for one more burst of help from Henry. The hold on her ankle loosened, and gathering her last shred of energy, she gave a powerful thrust with her other leg.

She was free! Luke dragged her upward, and she kicked with frantic urgency. Every cell in her body blared warning sirens, demanding oxygen. Her head broke the surface, and she gasped, sucking air into her burning lungs.

"I've got you," Luke said, treading water as he helped support her. "Just breathe."

She couldn't answer beyond her desperate, wheezing breaths. Dizziness engulfed her, and she splashed her limbs, terrified of slipping under again. From somewhere far away, she could hear Alice calling out, the words indistinguishable, the tone shrill with concern.

"Just relax. I'll get us back. I just need you to roll onto your back and float, okay?"

She could trust him. Fighting the instinct to struggle, she allowed him to maneuver her onto her back. The sunlight stabbed at her eyes and she squeezed them shut. Luke locked one strong arm around her upper body, and as he towed her, she drifted, inhaling lungfuls of precious air.

CHAPTER 22

*H*e swam toward the bank, his muscles churning through the water, fueled by adrenaline and fear. Was she really okay? He summoned another burst of speed, desperate to get her to shore. When it got too shallow to swim, he scooped her up and carried her. Gram waded in, her hands fluttering with the need to help, but there was nothing she could do but murmur to Callie as he lurched awkwardly up the bank. A few feet away from the pond, he laid her down on the grass and dropped to his knees beside her. Gram knelt on her other side.

"Please be okay," he rasped, smoothing her wet hair away from her frighteningly pale face.

Her eyes fluttered open, and she squinted in the glare of the sun. "I'm okay," she said, her voice weak but steady.

He shifted, positioning his body to shade her face. "Are you sure? Just rest." He grabbed her hand and squeezed gently.

"I'll go get towels and blankets," said Gram, pushing herself up to standing. "Should I call an ambulance?"

"Yes," he replied, at exactly the same time as Callie said, "No." He ground his teeth together. "Just bring your phone with you when you come back, Gram. Okay? Mine is somewhere in the pond, and I'm sure Callie's is too." He knew he should be the one running up to the house to grab what they needed—he was faster and the hill was steep. But he just wasn't going to leave Callie's side. Not happening.

Callie rolled toward him, grabbing his arm. Her eyes were wide, the whites tinged with a network of pink lines. "There's a car. In the pond."

"I know, honey. I saw it go in. It's okay."

She shook her head, her cold fingertips pressing into his flesh. "No, not mine. Another car."

"What?" The slam of a car door echoed from up near the house, and he glanced to the top of the hill. Cursing inwardly, he blew out a breath. His parents were here. He turned back to Callie. "Just lie back, okay?"

She ignored him. "There's another car down there! I saw it, when we were sinking. It has to be Blair's. She said she was here, and that's what she meant. In the pond!"

What? What did she mean, when *we* were sinking? "Slow down, honey. Take a breath."

Nodding, she gulped in air, keeping her gaze on his. "Blair's ghost was in the backseat of my car. She took control of my car, and drove it into the pond. The brakes wouldn't work. The doors wouldn't open." Her voice broke on a sob, and she closed her eyes for a moment.

Fury built as she relayed the details of her ordeal, and he had to keep reminding himself not to clench her hand too hard as his muscles tensed. Behind him, he could hear the buzz of frantic conversation as his parents and Gram hurried down the hill. Callie struggled to sit up as they approached, and he bit down on the urge to argue, helping support her instead.

"Oh my God!" his mother cried, clutching at her chest. High-heeled shoes dangled from her other hand. "Is everyone all right?"

Gram waved her cell phone. "We need to call an ambulance," she said as she thrust it into John's hand, taking a blanket from him in exchange. She circled around behind Callie and settled it around her shoulders.

Callie shook her head as she clutched at the blanket. "No, we need to call the police. There's a car in the pond. Another car, I mean, besides mine. I think it belongs to Blair, and I think her body is inside it."

A chorus of gasps and questions blended into one another, until his mother raised her voice above the din. "What makes you think that, Callie?"

"She's a psychic, Mom. We asked you both to come over here tonight so we could tell you everything that's been going on. I know it's a lot to take in right now, but Hillwood is being haunted by a very...violent ghost." He decided not to mention Pop for now. "We have reason to believe it's Blair. That's she's dead, and her body is here," he finished grimly, nodding toward the pond.

"That's not possible," his mother insisted in a strange

tone that seemed to dare someone to challenge her assertion.

His father cleared his throat. "Yes, it is."

A stunned silence fell around them. Luke finally broke it. "What do you mean, Dad? Do you know something about Blair?"

John shot a look at his wife. "If you don't tell them, I will. It's time."

Cynthia's expression hardened as she stared at him. "John..." She trailed off with a heavy sigh.

Gram held up her hands. "Clearly, we all have a lot to talk about. But not here. Callie's been through a horrible accident, and she's soaked. Let's all go up to the house, get her some dry clothes, and then we can decide what to do. And who to call."

As usual, once she'd made up her mind, Gram's voice held that steely conviction her family rarely argued with. Luke helped Callie up, and they all made their way back up the hill.

CHAPTER 23

*A*s Callie lowered herself into the chair, she had an eerie sense of déjà vu. Here she was again, exhausted after a traumatic event, sitting in the farmhouse, a hot toddy in front of her. This time she was at the dining table, a repeat of the family dinner except for the absence of Ryan. And there was no food on the table, just the drinks Alice had made for everyone. She noticed that John and Cynthia just had tumblers of whiskey instead of the warm mixture in her mug. Both of Luke's parents looked miserable, faces drawn, mouths tight.

"Mom and Dad, I think you should start," Luke said. "We need to hear what you know about Blair."

He'd pulled her chair right next to his, and his arm was slung around her shoulders in a protective embrace. She leaned into his body, beyond caring what anyone thought.

John and Cynthia exchanged a glance, and then Cynthia turned toward her son. "You have to understand, Luke. We didn't want this to affect you."

"What, exactly?"

John touched his wife's arm before taking a swig of his drink. "I'll do it."

Cynthia sniffled, nodding.

"It was early March, when Mom and Pop—Alice and Henry—were on the cruise." John gestured toward Alice. "And Luke was staying here, taking care of the animals." He brought his gaze back to Luke. "One evening, you called to ask if your mother or I could come by the farm, to let the dog out. You had something for work, and you didn't think Petey could make it until you got home without going out."

"I remember." Luke's fingers tightened on her shoulder.

"We came over together, I'd say it was around 5:30. And when we parked, we heard a noise coming from inside the garage. An engine, running." John paused for another drink. "We went in to check."

Callie glanced at Luke. She could see he knew where this was going, as did she, and dread pulsed through her.

"Blair's car was in there, and she was inside. Dead. It was suicide, Luke, no question. On her lap was a note that said, 'Dear Luke, look what you did.'"

Callie's stomach heaved. "Oh, my God," she whispered.

Luke remained silent, his expression stony.

"I don't know how she got in," John continued. "Maybe a door was open, or a window. Knowing her, she could have stolen a key and copied it. But we didn't want you to find her there, and we didn't want you to know what she'd done."

"So you...drove her car into the lake?"

"You would have blamed yourself!" Cynthia stifled a sob, her manicured fingers covering her mouth.

Luke tensed. "You don't know what I would have done. This was about you. You didn't want anyone to know."

Cynthia slapped her hands down on the table. "That girl put you through hell. She ruined *all* our lives for months. We were not going to let her do it forever. It was her choice to kill herself, and that decision was not something that should have any impact on our family."

Callie hesitated for a beat, then plunged in, hoping to keep things between Luke and his mother from escalating. "So, Blair was angry that Luke wasn't the one to find her, after everything she'd planned. Angry that he didn't even know she was dead, and that her body had been hidden. And then I showed up here, and her rage just spiraled. I became the perfect target."

Confusion clouded both of Luke's parents' faces, and she realized they really didn't know the rest of the story— the dual haunting, or the deadly situations their actions had unleashed. A wave of weariness swept over her, and she turned to Luke for help.

John cleared his throat. "So you expect us to believe Blair's ghost has been haunting this place since she died?"

A muscle in Luke's jaw twitched. "I don't expect you to believe anything. I'll tell you both exactly what's been happening, though. I realize you don't really know Callie, but you do know Gram and me, so you should keep that in mind while you're listening to what we have to say."

As Luke spoke, Callie took small sips of her drink, letting the honey and whiskey spread warmth through her bones. Her body ached and her mind felt woozy, but she was strangely alert, as though she'd traveled so far beyond exhaustion, she'd come full circle back to wide awake. She was content to let Alice and Luke relate the details of the past few weeks, and she only answered questions addressed directly to her. But she chimed in toward the end of the surreal story, when Henry's name came up again.

"I think Henry's death was so sudden, and so far away from home, that he just wasn't ready to move on. His spirit was drawn to Hillwood, his lifelong home, the place where his wife still lived. When he encountered Blair's ghost here, he realized she meant to make trouble for his family. And then he had to stay, to try to protect his loved ones from the anger and vengeance he sensed was coming."

"And he saved you," Luke said, his voice thick with emotion.

"You both saved me."

Cynthia wiped at her moist eyes, leaving smoky trails of smeared mascara. "What now? Do we have to call the police?"

"I think we do," Luke said, reaching for Callie's hand.

"This won't be good for the family," Cynthia said. "Your father's practice…"

Alice's mug thumped against the table as she set it down. "I'll take the blame. What can they do to an old woman?"

Luke shook his head. "Gram, you weren't even here when it happened. And we're not letting you do that anyway."

"Blame it on me. It was my idea, and that's the truth. I pushed John into it." Cynthia's tone turned defiant. "I was trying to protect my son."

John dragged his hand over his haggard face. "We both were. We were in shock."

"Oh, John." Alice sighed, resting her elbows on the table and cradling her head in her hands.

"I'll take the blame," Cynthia repeated.

"Failure to report a body is a misdemeanor, at most. But...I know people in high places. We didn't kill anyone. We'll get it figured out, quickly and quietly."

"Will it...be over then? The haunting?" Alice asked, her voice wavering.

All four of them turned their gazes on Callie, and she shrugged, squirming in her seat. "Um...I don't think she cares about legalities. She killed herself. I think what really matters is giving her a proper burial. Reuniting her with her family. And recognizing the pain she was in." She glanced at Luke. "Maybe Luke can go to her funeral and say goodbye, and offer a few kind words."

His grip on her hand tightened. "You can't be serious." He paused, blowing out a breath. "No, you're right. I'll do whatever it takes to keep you safe. To keep everyone safe."

"I think it will work," she said softly, giving his hand a squeeze back.

"I hope so. Mom and Dad, I need you to stay with Gram for now, though. Either here or at your place. I'm taking Callie to the hospital. You all can start making calls."

"No, Luke. I'm fine, really."

He turned to her, his blue eyes dark with worry. "Callie,

I need to know you're okay. I mean, I need to hear it from a doctor." He cupped his palm around her cheek. "Please. I love you, and I need to make sure you're okay."

Her breath hitched. Had he really just said he loved her? In front of his family? Tears welled in her eyes, blurring his handsome face momentarily. Swallowing, she blinked them away. "I love you, too."

The scrape of Alice's chair preceded her voice. "Let's give them a few minutes," she suggested, ushering John and Cynthia out of the room.

CHAPTER 24

*C*allie was lying on the bed in her room at Hillwood, playing a word game on her phone and waiting for Luke's call, when the voice murmured in her head. Henry's voice.

She's gone.

Callie froze, nerves crackling like live wires. Did that mean what she hoped it meant? Today was Blair's funeral, and Luke was in Florida, doing his part to try to put her to rest for once and all. Mrs. Adams had made the arrangements, and when he'd told her he intended to fly down for the service, he'd asked if he could also say a few words.

He'd wanted Callie to travel with him at first, but they'd both realized it was a bad idea. It was only one night, and although nothing strange or frightening had happened since the pond incident, neither of them wanted Alice to be alone at Hillwood, just in case. And they agreed the less Callie was involved in this part of encouraging Blair to move on, the better.

"I'm listening," she whispered into the silence of the room.

I...go too now. The words faded in and out, like a bad cell phone connection, and her head pulsed with a corresponding ache. But she didn't think the lack of clarity was due to another spirit's interference. It felt different, as though Henry himself was fading, losing strength finally after his efforts to hang on so long.

Tell...love them. Tell Alice she will always...love of my life.

Her phone rang, and she nearly levitated off the bed. "I will, Henry. I will. Rest in peace now, and thank you." She squeezed her eyes shut for a moment before sliding her finger across the screen. "Hi," she said a bit breathlessly, praying he would confirm what his Pop had just told her.

"Everything okay there, beautiful?"

Her heart swelled at the sound of Luke's voice. "Yes. How did it go?"

"It went well," he said, exhaling. The sound of a car starting floated through the phone. "The service was nice. I stood up and said everything we discussed. I hope it worked."

She sat up, turning to peer out the window. Shafts of evening sunlight broke through the clouds to stretch across the surface of the pond. "I think it did."

ALTHOUGH HE TOLD her not to, she waited up for him to return home. Wrapped in a blanket, she sat on the farmhouse porch, listening to the sounds of the night around her. Moths danced around the outdoor lights, mimicking the butterflies tumbling through her stomach. After so much time spent together, just being away from Luke for one night had felt like torture. She didn't want to think about what would happen now, though. The danger—hopefully—was over. Her apartment would be ready in a few weeks. The circumstances that had held them together would no longer exist. What would happen then?

Headlights swept up the driveway, and she jumped from the rocking chair, sending it swaying wildly. Her bare feet padded softly against the weathered boards as she rounded the corner and flew down the steps.

The door to his truck slammed, and he caught her in his arms as they met at the edge of the side porch stairs. Wordlessly, he lifted her into the air, burying his face in her neck.

"I'm so happy you're home!" she cried, breathing in his scent.

"Me too, beautiful. God, I missed you." He set her down and kissed her hungrily. "I told you not to wait up, but I'm glad you did."

"Yeah?"

"Yeah," he replied, his voice rough. "Let's go upstairs." He pulled her toward the house.

She laughed. "Do you want to maybe get your bag?"

"It's not high on my priority list." But he released her and strode around to the backseat of the truck. "Don't go anywhere."

"I won't."

When he returned, he set his duffle bag on the pavement and took both her hands in his. In the shadowy light, his playful expression turned serious. "Callie, I don't want this to end. I'm glad the bad stuff is over, but I don't want *this* to be over." He squeezed her fingers. "You and me."

Her chest contracted. She didn't know what to say. Even if she did, she wasn't sure she could speak. Somehow she'd let herself fall, despite the danger to her heart. And now, she would have to make an agonizing choice. His words filled her with both joy and fear, and she trembled as her emotions battled.

"I want us to be together," he added, dipping his head to meet her gaze.

She swallowed. "I want that too. But I'm scared."

"I know. But you're the bravest woman I know. And the kindest, smartest, and funniest." He pulled her into an embrace, trailing his lips over her ear. "And the sexiest."

She shivered with pleasure even as uncertainty coursed through her. He wanted their relationship to continue. To grow. This was her chance to stop it before it went any further. She could walk away—accept the pain now rather than risk absolute devastation if something bad happened in the future.

If she ended it now, she'd be hurting him, too. But didn't he deserve better than her? She pulled away until she could look up into his face. "We've only known each other a few weeks," she pointed out.

"We've been through more in the past three weeks than most couples go through in a year. And we'll get closer with every day we spend together."

That's what I'm afraid of. "I come with a lot of baggage."

"I've got some of my own, remember? But it's all out in the open already. We can handle it." He rubbed his hand across her back. "Callie, you're not going to come up with an argument to change my mind."

"I won't travel on highways in bad weather," she blurted out.

"That just makes good sense."

"I don't like crowded places."

He chuckled softly. "I'm fine with that. This is what I love." Reaching an arm out, he gestured to the surrounding fields and woods, cloaked in darkness, still and quiet beneath a dome of stars. "And you. I love you. I'm hoping one day, you'll be living here with me. Permanently."

Her heart swelled as she leaned back into him. "I love you, too."

"Will you give us a chance, then?"

Could she do it? Open herself up completely? Hold nothing back, despite her fears?

She could try. She would try. "Yes."

ABOUT THE AUTHOR

Kathryn Knight spends a great deal of time in her fictional world, where mundane chores don't exist and daily life involves steamy romance, dangerous secrets, and spooky suspense. Her novels are award-winning #1 Amazon and Barnes & Noble Bestsellers and RomCon Reader-Rated picks. When she's not reading or writing, Kathryn spends her time catching up on those mundane chores, driving kids around, and teaching fitness classes. She lives on beautiful Cape Cod with her husband, their two sons, and a number of rescued pets.

Please visit her at www.kathrynknightbooks.blogspot.com, or on social media at Kathryn Knight Books

FaceBook page or @k_knightbooks.

AN EXCERPT FROM GULL HARBOR BY KATHRYN KNIGHT

CHAPTER 1

THE WORDS DRIFTED with the dust motes across the dimly lit tavern. "Can I help you?"

That voice. Claire Linden froze in the doorway, her eyes struggling to adjust to the shadows. The dazzling Cape Cod sunshine still warmed her back as her gaze swept the cool darkness of the room.

She knew it was him before her gaze found him at a corner table, his long legs propped up, his attention focused on a computer screen. Even after five years, she would recognize Max's deep voice anywhere. That voice had sung her a million songs, moaned her name in the heat of passion, and whispered promises of love in her ear.

Claire slapped her sunglasses on her face with a trembling hand as he lifted his head and flicked a glance in her direction. She pictured his familiar eyes—an impossible shade of blue that contrasted sharply with his black hair—sweeping over her. Would he recognize her?

"We're closed right now. Starting Memorial Day weekend we'll be open for lunch." He smiled apologetically and returned to his work.

Nodding, she backed out the door and let it swing shut. She drew in a ragged breath as she collapsed against the faded wooden shingles of the alcove. What was Max Baron doing in this sleepy beachside town?

She wasn't sure if she was relieved or hurt that he hadn't recognized her. Tugging a damp hand through her long hair, she studied the color of the wavy strands. It was now a rich burgundy, a big change from the chocolate brown it had been in college. And she had shed her preppy attire for a more bohemian style. Today, a strappy white tank top hugged her upper body while a summery skirt floated around her calves.

These alterations were intentional and calculated. She was embarking on her career as a paid medium, and she wanted to look the part. People didn't expect a woman who communicated with ghosts to dress conservatively. Her tight budget didn't allow for many clothing purchases, but over the years she had managed to create a wardrobe suitable for a professional clairvoyant.

Oddly enough, it was Max who had convinced her to embrace her gift; to abandon her father's plan in order to follow her own dreams. Then Max had suddenly abandoned her, and all their plans, without even a hint of an explanation. A fresh wave of betrayal tore through her, threatening to rip open old wounds.

She pushed herself away from the wall and ordered her feet to move. It didn't matter why he was here. She was here to do a job; to prove to herself, and her father, that she could make it on her own.

A wry smile tugged at her lips at that thought. Her father had cut her off, financially and emotionally, when she had announced that she wouldn't be attending law school. Judge Linden wouldn't know if she were lying dead in a ditch, much less succeeding as a medium. Still, she had her pride to consider, and bills to pay.

Closed stores lined the sidewalk of Main Street, and she glanced through the windows of antique shops and art galleries as she walked, looking for signs of life. Although it wasn't officially summer, there had to be someone around who could give her directions. Someone other than Max.

Crossing the side street, she spotted another restaurant that looked promising. A sign welcomed her to Gull Harbor Diner and a tinkling bell announced her presence as she pulled open the glass door. There were no other patrons at the moment, but the atmosphere was bright and cheery, a sharp contrast to the hazy tavern where she had inexplicably encountered her college boyfriend.

Suddenly exhausted, she slid onto a bright red vinyl stool at the long counter as a smiling man appeared from the kitchen. He greeted her with a friendly, "What can I get you?" as he made his way to the end of the counter to stand across from her. His dusty brown hair was just beginning to grey at the temples, and his warm hazel eyes shone with kindness.

She wasn't really hungry. "Just coffee would be great."

He nodded, pulling a white mug from beneath the counter. "We brew the best coffee in town. Much better than that fancy coffee house franchise they're trying to open here." Giving her a companionable wink, he poured the dark liquid into her cup. "I wish them luck. We don't do chains around here, never have."

"I noticed. It's very quaint here," she said sincerely as she accepted the cream and sugar.

"You're visiting us for the first time then? I'm certain I would remember having seen such a pretty face before."

Claire smiled weakly and took a tentative sip from the steaming mug. "Thank you. Actually, I'm staying here for the summer. I could use some directions, if you know how to get to Mill Pond Road."

His expression turned serious. "You're not looking for the old Williams house, are you?"

"No, the owners' last name is Llewellyn."

He shook his head, a frown clouding his pleasant features. "Same place. Until recently, that property belonged to the Williams family as far back as the 1950s. You're not staying there alone, are you?"

She ignored the question, countering with one of her own instead. "You've heard something about the house?"

"Nothing good. And I hear more gossip than anyone around here, except maybe Max."

"Max?" she asked, struggling to keep her voice casual.

"Oh, sorry, of course you don't know him. Max Baron owns the local watering hole."

"Fantastic," she muttered.

"What's that?"

She cast her gaze about wildly and found a wall clock, its decorative hands represented by a fork and knife. "The time," she said. "I really need to get going. What do I owe you?" Gulping down the last of her coffee in an attempt to appear as though she truly was in hurry, she reached for her purse.

"No charge," he insisted, extending his hand. "Name's Dan O'Brien. Welcome to Gull Harbor. You should come by in the morning for breakfast, that's when we're busiest."

"Claire Linden," she said, sliding her hand into his. "And thanks very much, I just might do that. Do you think you could give me directions to the Llewellyn house?"

"Of course I *can*, I just don't really want to. But since you're obviously the psychic they hired to investigate the house, I assume you have other methods of getting the information, even if I refuse."

"Don't worry, I can't read people's minds," she said, laughing at his relieved expression. "I really would appreciate the help; I was driving around those back roads for an hour—they all look the same, and there seems to be a serious lack of street signs in the area." She looked at Dan hopefully, armed with a pen and a napkin.

He sighed. "Fine, but I'm going to give you my phone number just in case there's trouble. I'm not saying I believe that house is haunted, but I've heard a lot of disturbing rumors lately."

Was he truly worried about a complete stranger, or was he hitting on her? She decided to give him the benefit of the doubt and accepted the phone number along with the directions. After thanking him for his help, she hurried to her car, carefully keeping her face turned away as she passed the windows of Max's tavern.

SHE DETECTED the presence behind her a moment before a sharp sting of pain bit into her shoulder. "Ow!" she yelled, her surprised cry echoing through the secluded woods that surrounded the house. Whirling around, she raked her eyes over the untamed yard that stretched toward the road.

Only silent scrub pines and thorny brambles returned her gaze. But a jagged rock lay at her feet. Claire reached around to gingerly probe the tender skin of her back. Wincing, she pulled her hand back and examined the streak of bright blood that smeared her fingertips.

It was starting already. There was no point in wandering around, peering behind trees—she knew that whatever had thrown the rock had no need for hiding spots. She picked up the rock and rubbed it between her palms. "I'm here to help you," she called out in a soothing voice.

Turning slowly, she repeated her message to the abandoned house. Only a few nervous bird calls broke the silence as she walked toward the front porch of the

Llewellyns' retirement home. The sweet old couple had put all their money into purchasing the property at auction. Then they had endured three months of aggressive paranormal activity before they had finally fled in terror.

Claire no longer felt anything other than a profound loneliness that seemed to emanate from the house. She set the rock on the porch steps and fished in her pocket for the key. The front door opened to reveal the hallmark center staircase of a Cape style house.

She wandered into the great room, her eyes falling on a pile of frames heaped in the middle of the floor. Squatting down, she turned one over with a slightly shaky hand. Two little girls—grandchildren, most likely—smiled from behind the glass. In another photograph, she recognized the Llewellyns. They were standing on the beach in happier times.

With a frown, she stood up and rubbed her throbbing shoulder. All the pictures were face down, and Claire highly doubted this was Mrs. Llewellyn's idea of a decorating statement. She propped two of the frames back on tables before she continued on to the kitchen.

Nothing seemed amiss in the kitchen and dining areas, but the master bedroom was a scene of destruction. More picture frames littered the floor, and smashed glass crunched beneath her sandals. The bed was unmade, and clothes spilled from open drawers. She caught her reflection in a cracked mirror that hung askew on the wall; several pairs of her green eyes stared out at her from the jagged slivers. She shuddered and continued on her tour.

Trailing her hand along the worn banister, she climbed

the staircase. Each step made a different creaking noise, reminding her of an eerie xylophone. There was a bathroom at the top of the stairs and a room to each side of the hallway.

She took a tentative step into the room to her left. Boxes and odd pieces of furniture were amassed in the corners, and a few dusty cobwebs hung from the ceiling. On the floor was a loose mound of sticks and leaves. Something about the odd pile of debris in the center of the empty room struck her as more disturbing than the chaos downstairs. Nausea bubbled up in her stomach, and she backed out of the room slowly.

Across the hallway, a more pleasant room featured a queen-sized bed, a painted wooden dresser, and a rocking chair with a nautical-themed pillow. She nodded in approval; this is where she would sleep. Peering out the back window, she admired the western edge of Mill Pond, sparkling behind the trees.

The house's proximity to both the kettle pond and the Cape Cod National Seashore had surely been the reason the Llewellyns had sunk their meager life savings into this property. Claire silently prayed that she would succeed in ridding their home of the angry spirit that was making their life here unbearable. Mr. Llewellyn had told her that retiring to the idyllic coastal town of Gull Harbor had been their dream.

Had living here been Max's dream as well? If so, he had never mentioned it to her. Just add it to the list of things he'd kept from her, she thought with a wry smile. Anyway, it hardly mattered now. Claire tossed her shoulders back, sending up a flare of pain from her cut. She had a job to do here, she reminded herself as she hurried down the musical staircase. An important job that had absolutely nothing to do with Max. Hopefully this small town would be big enough for the two of them.

Printed in Great Britain
by Amazon